Mountain Bike Mayhem

Books in the Choice Adventures series

1 *The Mysterious Old Church*
2 *The Smithsonian Connection*
3 *The Underground Railroad*
4 *The Rain Forest Mystery*
5 *The Quarterback Sneak*
6 *The Monumental Discovery*
7 *The Abandoned Gold Mine*
8 *The Hazardous Homestead*
9 *The Tall Ship Shakedown*
10 *The Class Project Showdown*
11 *The Silverlake Stranger*
12 *The Counterfeit Collection*
13 *Mountain Bike Mayhem*
14 *The Mayan Mystery*
15 *The Appalachian Ambush*
16 *The Overnight Ordeal*

Mountain Bike Mayhem

R. P. Proctor

Tyndale House Publishers, Inc.
Wheaton, Illinois

Copyright © 1994 by The Livingstone Corporation
All rights reserved
Cover illustration copyright © 1993 by John Walker

Library of Congress Cataloging-in-Publication Data

Proctor, R. P. (Roger P.)
  Mountain bike mayhem / R.P. Proctor.
    p. cm.—(Choice adventures ; #13)
  Summary: The reader's choices determine the course of action as a group
of Christian friends dodge a gang and a crazy old man while riding their
mountain bikes.
  ISBN 0-8423-5131-0
  1. Plot-your-own stories.   [1. Plot-your-own stories.
2. Adventure and adventures—Fiction.   3. Christian life—Fiction.]
I. Title. II. Series.
PZ7.P9423Mo 1994
[Fic]—dc20   93-38898

Printed in the United States of America

99 98 97 96 95 94
 9   8   7   6   5   4   3   2   1

Willy climbed the stairs of the apartment building slowly, letting his feet fall heavily on the steps. He knew it would be a long weekend with nothing to do while Chris and Pete were gone, and he did not look forward to getting it under way. Willy knew that right now Chris and Pete were watching the great flat table of Washington, D.C., drop away from their plane, on their way to a national science competition in Denver, Colorado, and Willy was stuck at home. Why couldn't *he* go on a trip?

He pushed open the door and peered into the kitchen. "Mom!" he yelled, but no one answered. "Zeke!" No answer. "Mom! Colleen! Hello!" No one was home. He dropped his knapsack heavily on the kitchen table and started rummaging through the refrigerator. "They must be down at the home," he said offhandedly to himself.

Willy poured a bowl of cereal and headed into the living room. He sat heavily on the couch and clicked on the tube. Just the same dull cartoon repeats. He stared blankly at the screen and chewed his cereal like a pig, intentionally making a mess on his face and the coffee table as he ate. And then it hit him. Why couldn't he go on a trip? Just because he couldn't go away to Denver with Chris didn't mean he had to mope around the house and make a mess—although the mess part was kind of fun. He slid the bowl of cereal down on the coffee table and scrambled for

2

the phone. Just because Chris and Pete left didn't mean everyone else had to stop what they were doing.

Willy dialed Sam's number and waited as the phone rang and rang. No one was answering. He put down the receiver and began dialing Chris's number automatically before he realized what he was doing. Putting the receiver down a little harder this time, Willy started muttering to himself. Grabbing the phone, he dialed Jim's number and started rocking in his chair and tapping his foot. "Where is everybody?"

Finally someone picked up the phone.

"Hello." It was Jim's grandmother.

"Hello, Mrs. Whitehead. Is Jim there?" he said excitedly.

"No," the older woman said. Her voice was its usual calm, shy whisper. "No, he just left with Sam and some other boy. They said they were going down to the Freeze to hang out. Can I take a message for him, Willy?"

"No, that's OK," Willy said disappointedly. "I wanted to do something. I'll just go down to the Freeze and find them there." He hung up and ran for the door. He bolted down the steps two by two and crashed out of the apartment, nearly falling to his knees. He slammed the door behind him and jumped on his bike in one move and was pedaling fast down the driveway.

When Willy got to the Common he could see Sam's and Jim's bikes propped outside the Freeze. He pedaled faster and came to a sliding stop just outside the door. Inside he could see the others look up from their comics at the counter. There were Jim and Sam, just as he expected, and another kid he had never seen before with them.

"Hey!" Willy yelled as he climbed off his bike and set it against the building. "Come on out here you guys!"

The guys left the comics on the counter and came out into the sun. Sam was already dressed for a trip—jeans worn at the knees, sweatshirt, and a ball cap. He carried a red backpack that Willy knew was filled up with knee and arm pads and a helmet. None of them could afford to buy their own set of pads, so they chipped in and got an expensive set to share. But Jim was still wearing his clothes from school. And the new kid was wearing ratty clothes. Sam came out first. Jim stayed just inside the door with the new kid behind him.

"I expected you to beat us here and be pigging down some chocolate macadamia by now," Sam said grinning.

"Hey, Sam," Willy said, "I was just thinking about what to do for the weekend." Willy looked up into the sky. "Chris and Pete just left for that science competition." Willy put his arm out on Sam's shoulder and shook him a little bit as he spoke, for emphasis. "But why should we be stuck with boredom for the weekend? Who's the guy with Jim?"

Sam leaned close and said in a whisper, "That's a guy he met at school. He comes from Emeryville. Just like all the guys from that town, he doesn't have any money. Jim had to buy him some ice cream."

"Huh," Willy noted. "Where'd you bums get money?" He turned and peered into the Freeze. "Hey Jim!" he called past Sam. "Come here! We have some stuff to do!"

The new kid came out behind Jim, almost as a shadow hiding behind him. He was taller than Jim, and his trying to look smaller made him look funny. Willy smiled. The new

4

kid was pale, with reddish hair and bright blue eyes. His face was long and looked sad. He wore jeans with a hole in the left knee, a black T-shirt, and an old, worn, gray jacket that looked a size too big. He had his hands shoved deep into the pockets of his jacket.

"Who's the new guy?" Willy asked.

"This is the Bean Pole Jones." Sam thumbed over his shoulder with an accent. "Emeryville anorexic extraordinaire." The new kid turned red and looked down.

"No, seriously," Jim said, "this is Eric Donaldson. He's new at school. He buses in from Emeryville."

"So, you're from Emeryville, huh," Willy said. Most Millersburg kids thought that the guys from Emeryville were a bunch of dorks. Willy made a mental note about it. He had never actually known anyone from Emeryville before—just heard stories.

"Yeah," Jim said a little more seriously, "but he's cool. What's up, Willy?"

"I was thinking about Chris and Pete getting to go all the way to Denver for the weekend and us being stuck here and it hit me: Why do *we* have to be stuck here? Why don't *we* do something interesting? Why don't *we* take a trip too? We can pull an all-nighter. We haven't done that in a long time."

The guys came over and leaned on their bikes as they talked—all except for the new guy, Eric. He just stood nearby and listened. Willy didn't know if he trusted him yet.

"Let's ride out to the Sinks," Willy said excitedly. "We can camp out on the shore. I can grab some franks at home and we can cook outside and—"

"Don't worry about hot dogs, Willy. You're hot dog enough for all of us." Sam laughed.

"Very funny," Willy said as he slapped Sam in the chest.

"I don't know if we should," said Jim. "Last time we pulled an all-nighter we all ended up in the custody of the FBI. Why don't we go do motocross at the Pits instead?"

Eric's eyes got big. "F-B-I?"

"Don't let it freak you out," Willy said. "Pete's dad is an agent. It's no big deal."

"Sinks or Pits?" Sam called out.

CHOICE➤

If you think they should go to the Sinks, turn to page 40.

If you think they should go to the Pits, turn to page 25.

6

We have to respect other people!" said Jim.

"I don't want to sound like Rev. Whitehead or anything, but this reminds me of that Bible verse, 'Do not judge unless you are judged.' " said Sam.

Willy laughed. "I don't think that's how it goes."

Sam punched him.

"It's more like, 'Do not judge, or you too will be judged,' " said Jim. "I think it's in Matthew."

"All right, Rev. Whitehead," Sam teased.

"So what does it mean?" asked Eric.

"In other words, don't," Sam began, fumbling for words, "don't . . ." Finally he said, *"I* don't know. Jim, what does it mean?"

Jim shrugged. "In other words, *we* don't know anything about this guy, so we shouldn't just assume that he's weird and get all over his face just because he freaked out Willy."

Willy shut his eyes and held his breath. Jim was right. What did he know about this old man? None of them got hurt. None of them got their bikes taken away. None of them really knew *anything* about this mystery guy—hardly anything at all. It was terribly tempting to *think* they had a right to the box, but in reality they didn't. No matter what it *looked* like. . . .

"Things aren't always what they seem," said Eric,

holding up his deformed hand and interrupting Willy's
thoughts. "People see my hand, think I'm retarded or a
freak or something, and ..."

Sam, Willy, and Jim all nodded knowingly. "...and get it
all wrong!" finished Sam.

Willy stood there and prayed. *Please Lord, forgive me
for judging this old man ...and jumping to conclusions—
again.* While he was praying, he made up his mind. "OK,
moto-kings, let's get this box back to where we found it."

Jim piled the box onto Sam's handlebars, and the gang
rode back into the woods. Willy kept looking around,
checking for the old man, but they didn't see him again.
Once the box was in place, they stood staring at it. "Well,
what now?" asked Willy. All of the guys had lost their zest
for motocross and were starting to get hungry.

"Cowabunga!" Sam shouted, slapping his forehead,
"we forgot the barbecue!"

Jim and Willy gasped. "You're right!" They were
supposed to meet at Capitol Community Church for a
barbecue and had completely forgotten. They quickly
remounted their bikes and zoomed back, dragging Eric
along with them to see the church and get to know some
people. It wasn't long before they had forgotten about the
box of treasures they left behind.

The old man looked on as the troupe disappeared
into the evening, and breathed a sigh of relief.

8

THE END

Who was this old man? If you haven't found out, turn
back to page 5 and make different choices along the way.

Or, turn to page 141.

Shhh," Willy whispered softly. "Listen. If we try to get out now the old man will probably catch the last guy out. By the time the other two get help, who *knows* what the old man will do to his victim!" The other two guys settled down a little. "All we have to do is wait here."

"But Willy," said Jim, "we saw the boxes. What if he comes in for them?"

Willy didn't know. Maybe they would try to trip the man and get away, or hit him on the head, or plead with him. Willy didn't know. As they crouched there in the dark Willy prayed silently, *Please Lord, please don't let anything happen to us.*

"We'll pray, Jim," Willy said aloud.

The car door slammed and the old man moved into their vision. His back was to the cave opening as he gazed in the direction of the Sinks. Inside the cave the guys could hear the low thrum of a motorcycle approaching. Willy's heart sank. The old man was waiting for someone; he wasn't about to leave. When they heard the motorcycle, all three Ringers started to back further into the cave. To their amazement, it was deeper still. Soon the boxes they were crouching just behind were a good three yards in front of them, and they were deep inside the cave. The opening looked like a circle of light far away. And in the center of the circle stood the old man's silhouette.

10

From inside the cave they could see the motorcycle pull up. It was a police officer. Their hearts jumped. They were saved! As they watched, they anticipated the cop running off the old man from the area, maybe even arresting him once they showed him whatever was in the boxes. They watched breathlessly as the policeman climbed off his bike and walked over to the old man.

The old man and the cop shook hands.

"Oh no," whispered Jim. "What do we do now?"

"Get our bazookas," Sam joked. No one laughed.

"Nothing," Willy answered. They could see the two men talking, but they were too far away to hear what they were saying. After a second Willy turned to the others and whispered, "It doesn't look like they're coming this way. I'm going to move to the mouth to hear what they're saying."

"No! No!" the other two warned, but Willy had made up his mind. Slowly, silently, he crept toward the front of the cave. Sam and Jim began to get irritated at the way Willy was doing his own thing and not listening to them. As he approached, he could begin to make out what the two men were saying.

". . . fence," the old man finished.

"It doesn't make any difference to me," the cop replied. "They have to sell us the right materials, the marked stuff. Otherwise they could just say they were selling their own goods. At least we got them for buying. . . ." Their voices drifted off as they moved toward the old man's car. Willy motioned to the others to move up. They did.

"We can sneak outta here," Willy barely whispered, "if we just crawl along the base of the hill in the bushes. Move slowly so they don't hear you."

Jim motioned for Willy to lean close, as if he had a question or something. *"Bishshuhs,"* Willy sneezed right in Jim's face. The old man and the cop stopped dead in their tracks, wheeled around, and looked right at the guys.

CHOICE

If the guys separate, turn to page 129.

If they stick together, turn to page 32.

They watched as the other guys went upstairs. Right before Jim disappeared, he looked Willy in the eye. Jim was saying with his eyes, *Don't do it, Willy. Don't tell Sam!*

As soon as they were out of sight, Sam turned to Willy. "Well? What's the deal?"

"I found out about Eric," Willy said unexcitedly. "But I don't think I can tell you."

Sam looked shocked. "You mean you and Jim are going to keep a secret from *me?*"

"Look, Sam, you asked me to find out, so I did. Jim thinks that Eric will tell us all when he feels comfortable. He thinks it's his business; and we should respect that. It's really not so bad anyway, and—"

"Willy, I asked you to ask Jim so you could tell *me!* If it's not a big deal, then what's the problem?"

Willy sighed. "Let's just say Eric has a medical problem, and something else that Jim couldn't tell me."

Sam looked at him as if to say, *I can't believe you.* "I guess you and Jim can know, but not me, huh?"

Ouch. "Sam—" Willy began, but Sam reached down and grabbed the red knapsack and pushed past Willy with his bike. He left hurriedly through the fence and off down the street.

Willy kicked the dirt in exasperation. He stood there for a second, frustrated with himself for letting his curiosity ruin things. None of this would have happened if he and Sam hadn't plotted to pry out Eric's secrets in the first place.

Willy decided he had to apologize to Sam. He went over to the factory to tell the guys he had to patch up an argument with Sam, then rode slowly back to the Common, where he figured he'd find Sam. As he rode around he could see Sam's bike leaning against the front porch of the church.

He glanced at the town clock. It was nearly four-thirty. If he hurried, maybe there would still be time to apologize to Sam and be back for some motocross before dinner.

THE END

If you want to see how it could have turned out if Sam hadn't insisted on prying into Eric's secrets, turn to page 134 and make different choices along the way.

Or, turn to page 141.

Shaking his head, he said, "I can't. If you were in the same place, you wouldn't be able to either." He looked apologetically at Willy and walked away.

Willy stood shaking his head for a minute, unable to believe that Jim wouldn't tell him. What could possibly be so secret about Eric? "Hey you guys!" he yelled down the stairs, "let's stop messing around and get out there on the course!" He didn't wait for their reply, but headed right out onto the motocross course. He got out there, grabbed his bike, and started the first run without them to watch.

He decided to take the easy course first, just to warm up. It just went around over a few smaller hills. They set up that course when they were just kids. He rode it pretty hard, though, to work out his frustration. It felt pretty good, and when he cleared the last hill he could see Jim and Eric back out and stand there, waiting their turn. Eric was sitting on Jim's bike like he was going to go next.

"What's this?" Willy said as he came in to stop.

"In the factory, I talked Eric into doing the course," said Jim. "He was just a little off guard before."

"I can do it," Eric said with determination.

Now this is more like it, thought Willy. *Now we can get into what we're really here for.* "OK," Willy said as he dismounted his bike. "Where's Sam?"

"He's still back in the factory, sulking."

"Huh?" said Willy. "OK, go for it."

Eric stood and pedaled off, and Willy noticed he used only one hand to steer until he was almost out of sight. After Eric disappeared, Willy just went off by himself and let Jim sit in quiet.

Every once in a while, they could see Eric topping hills off in the Pits, and he was doing pretty well, too. Finally he crested the last hill, Boot Hill. Willy was shocked. Boot Hill was the biggest, steepest, baddest hill on the course. Willy wasn't at all surprised when Eric lost total control as he came down. Eric landed with a huge crash, but Jim's bike landed harmlessly in the weeds. Jim and Willy ran over. Willy stuck out his right hand and grabbed Eric's right arm to help him up. Halfway up, Willy noticed the deformity in Eric's hand—his little, gray, twisted hand had only three fingers. Willy let Eric go in shock, and Eric had to catch himself. Jim went around Willy and tried to help Eric up, who was still struggling to breathe from having the wind knocked out of him.

"Wow," Willy said below his breath. He could hear Sam coming up behind him just then. Willy didn't know whether to stop Sam to protect Eric's secret, or just ignore it and help like Jim was doing.

CHOICE ➡

If Willy decides to protect Eric's secret, turn to page 100.

If Willy decides just to help Eric get up, turn to page 61.

16

Willy decided not to talk to Eric. At least, not now. He just didn't know what to say. So he stayed where he was, looking out over the Pits, contemplating friendship.

There were three courses at the Pits that the guys had set up when they were kids. The first course was a simple figure eight with only two hills. They had done that when they were younger. They set up the other two courses after Chris got his new mountain bike on his last birthday.

None of them were really that familiar with the other courses. One was a huge circle around the Pits that went through several spots of shallow water. The other covered every hill they could make a path over and went continuously in and out of the trees. That was the Killer course, and it included Boot Hill.

Sam's run was over the Killer course, and he made pretty good time. Willy was next. He pulled on the gloves and pads they had brought in the red backpack and watched the guys out of the corner of his eye.

"Of course you knew I wouldn't be going on the Baby course," said Sam. "You guys have to follow the leader, so now that I have shown the way, we have to find out who the real men are."

Willy turned and smiled. The other guys were smiling too, except for Eric.

Willy shoved off and pedaled around a corner. He was

out of sight of the other guys, but that didn't matter to him. He didn't care about showing off the way Sam did. He just wanted to push it to the limit. The first couple hills were warm-ups, only about three yards high and not too steep. He climbed them easily and flew off their tops. Every once in a while he'd rip around a corner and appear in front of the guys, and they'd cheer.

The trail ducked into the woods on a narrow path. Willy couldn't see very far ahead, but he pedaled harder for the danger of plowing into something. As he rounded the corner, a dark figure suddenly loomed in the path. Willy gasped as an old man stood erect and turned his face toward the bike thundering down on him, his white hair a blur in Willy's vision as the hapless motocrosser sped uncontrollably ahead. The man jumped into the bushes just in time to avoid Willy as he wobbled wildly trying to regain control. "Hey!" yelled the man. In another wild second of crashing through bushes and nearly wiping out, Willy was out in the sun again.

Willy skidded to a dusty stop and looked back into the dark opening in the woods. Nothing. Not even movement.

Willy waited tensely at the mouth of the woods, ready to bolt if the man came out after him. He was breathing heavily, not sure what to do—go back in and see who that was, or go get the guys.

18

CHOICE ⇒

If Willy gets the guys, turn to page 103.

If Willy goes back into the woods, turn to page 77.

Willy had to think fast. He walked over to Eric. "Do you know why you can't really swim in the Dead Sink?" Eric shook his head. "Because it's polluted. That's the only reason. Sam made up the whole stupid story because that's what he does. He didn't mean to bust on you for your hand. He didn't mean it."

Eric pulled out his right hand and looked at it. Jim and Sam came over and watched. "You know," Eric finally said, "I've been hiding this thing for as long as I can remember. I was born this way. And every time I meet new people, which is a lot, I always do the same thing." He stuffed his hands in his pockets as he spoke.

"Sam," Eric said slowly, "you're a jerk. But you're a *funny* jerk. Jim warned me about you." Eric stood and walked over to Sam and, without a word, stuck out his right hand.

At first Sam didn't know what to do. But then he reached out and took Eric's hand. They shook.

When they were done, Sam looked at his own fingers. "He didn't take any!" he said, laughing. Willy smacked him in the arm.

"What did you mean when you said you meet a lot of new people?" Jim asked Eric as they all began again to get ready to swim.

Willy noticed a change in Eric's attitude since the

whole episode with Sam. He seemed more open and less secretive.

"Well," Eric began, "my mom and two younger sisters and I move around a lot. She always seems to have to find new jobs to support the family. The law won't let me work yet because I'm not old enough. But as soon as I can I will, to help out. She works all day and all night."

"Did something happen to your dad? Where is he?" Jim said.

"He's in Florida. That's where he left us when I was really little. That's where we started, and we've been moving up the coast ever since. I figure we'll keep going until Maine."

"You can get your first job on a lobster boat. They make a ton of money," said Sam.

"What do *you* know about lobster boats?" Willy asked sarcastically.

Sam thought for a second, then shrugged. "They float."

"So why do you come to school in our town instead of Emeryville?" Jim asked.

"That doesn't matter," Eric replied. "What I want to know is what that bus is doing in the water."

All the guys started over toward the Dead Sink. "That's not really a school bus," Willy answered. "That's some old hippie bus from prehistoric times. I think it even has flowers painted on it."

"Sick," Eric said with a wince. "Who in their right mind would paint flowers on a car?"

"Crazy people and communists," Sam said. "That's

what my parents always say about hippies." Everybody
laughed.

"So no one ever goes into the Dead Sink?" Eric asked.

The Ringers shook their heads.

Turn to page 37.

Willy cleared his throat and prepared the most pleasant, conciliatory tone he could muster: "What do you guys use the building for?"

"What's it to you, puke?" the big one barked. Without warning, the big one grabbed Eric. The other two Vipers reached for Willy and Sam, who jumped in fear and yelled out, "Aack!" Jim started backing away and started to run.

"Aye!"

Jim was stopped in his tracks with the sound of someone hitting the pavement. He became sickened at the thought of Willy, Sam, or Eric getting beaten up, and then suddenly became more concerned about his friends than himself. He turned around to help fight the Vipers, hoping not to have to face a knife or a gun.

To his surprise, the big Viper was lying on the floor with his face in the dust, Eric standing over him. The other Vipers had stopped to look, too, with their fists clenched around Willy and Sam's collars. All eyes were fixed on Eric, their amazement freezing the action.

Without a word, Eric turned to Viper number two and sent a kick to his midsection before the gang member could even respond. He crumpled to the floor.

Viper number three moved toward Eric to fight back, but Eric planted a punch to his face, causing the tough-looking guy to stagger back.

Jim, Willy, and Sam stood blinking, stunned. They only looked on as the moaning Vipers staggered around. Eric backed away from them and rejoined the Ringers.

The Vipers regrouped quickly and came all at once at the guys. This time they picked up stuff to hit with. Willy, Jim, Sam, and Eric turned and ran.

They ran like crazy down the stairs to get away from the gang that followed. They made a line for the door and came crashing through—right into the broad chest of a man who was coming in.

The boys piled into him, but the guy didn't even move. Looking up, the stranger seemed to be about ten feet tall, with white hair and piercing blue eyes. They were trapped between this stranger and the Vipers that were right behind them.

"What are you kids doing here?" the old man barked down on them.

"We're trying to leave!" said Eric.

"Well *do* it then, and don't come back!"

The guys got up and ran around the huge man. To Willy's astonishment, the Vipers had disappeared. Racing to their bikes, they grabbed them and pushed off across the Pits, all the while expecting the Vipers to pop up somewhere. All they could see back at the factory was the man standing on the landing, watching as they got their stuff together and left.

The ride back to town was an energetic discussion of what had happened.

"Why didn't the Vipers come after us after they saw

that guy there?" said Sam. "They were right behind us; they had to have seen him!"

"It was like they turned and ran from him as soon as they saw him," said Eric over Jim's shoulder on their one bike.

"Maybe he's one of them," said Willy, "the Viper Grand Wizard or something."

"If he was, then he was the granddaddy of gang guys if ever there was one," said Sam.

Willy shook his head as they headed back to the Freeze. What a weird afternoon!

When they got to the Freeze, they decided it would be better for their health if they stayed away from the Pits for a while.

THE END

If you haven't found out who the old man is, turn to page 40 and follow the story.

Otherwise, turn to page 141.

"Maybe Jim is right," Willy said, "and besides, Eric is only visiting for the day, so I don't think he can pull an all-nighter."

"Oh, I could," Eric said, obviously trying to not look like a dork. "There's no reason I can't stay out. I do it all the time."

"Well," Jim said, shaking his head, "I can't. If I get caught fooling around at night again, I won't get to go anywhere for a long time. Let's go to the Pits."

"What do you mean, *again?*" asked Willy.

"Air and Space Museum?"

"Oh, yeah."

Eric looked confused and shook his head. "To start with, what are the Pits?"

Sam turned and smiled as he explained. "The Pits are where they dumped the toxic waste from the factory. All kinds of rabid mutant animals live there. Crockamonkies. Tarantugeckos. That kind of stuff. We go down and ride the trails in between the mountains of toxic waste drums." The Ringers cracked up, all except for Willy.

"They don't have toxic waste in a furniture factory, you idiot," he said.

"Yeah, we haven't done motocross in months," Sam said. "Let's just go see if there isn't any."

"No, no, no," said Willy. "Two of our key moto-animals are gone, so I say we pull an all-nighter."

Sam and Willy looked hard at each other and squared off. "Just because Chris is gone doesn't make you the boss," said Sam.

"Well, I don't hear you coming up with anything exciting to do. What's exciting about motocross? We've done that a million times."

"Who feels like going out in the middle of nowhere and sleeping on the ground?"

Jim stepped in. "Wait a minute. Wait a minute. Let's vote on it. There are three of us—that's enough for a vote."

Sam liked the idea, but Willy didn't. "To heck with a vote. I say we pull an all-nighter."

"Vote!" said Sam.

"Vote!" said Jim.

"OK, OK," Willy gave in. "We'll vote on it."

The Ringers stood in a circle. Eric stood off to the side.

"Pits."

"Pits."

Sam and Jim looked at Willy. Willy's face seemed to darken as he thought of what to do.

CHOICE ⇦

If Willy decides to join in, turn to page 57.

If Willy decides to quit, turn to page 80.

Y ou've seen motocross on TV, haven't you?" Sam said, his voice prodding Eric. Willy thought Sam was in rare form today—Mr. Peer-Pressure.

"If he doesn't want to ride yet, let him just look around," Jim said.

"No," Eric spoke up, "I can ride. It's just that my bike is a little smaller than Sam's. And I want to see the track. . . ."

"Ba-cahck!" Sam said.

"I'm not a chicken," Eric said, stepping forward. He reached out for the bike with his left hand and pulled it away from Sam. Eric turned his body away from the guys and pushed the bike about ten yards from where they stood. After fumbling around with something in his pocket, he climbed onto the bike and pedaled clumsily around the corner that Sam had just ridden around. After a long, quiet moment, Sam turned to Willy and Jim.

"Jim, where'd you find this guy, anyway? He gives me the creeps."

"He's been in my class since September," Jim answered. "He never really talks to anyone and he looks miserable all the time, so I started inviting him over after school. He never said yes, until today."

"I don't know about this guy," Willy said. "Maybe the reason he's weird is because he's from Emery—"

A wild scream came from the top of the hill Sam had

just flown over. The three guys turned and looked up into the sky. Eric came flying over the top, a look of terror on his face. The bike seemed to have come loose from his grip and was falling away from his body. It wasn't the near-controlled flight that Sam had just pulled off; Eric's arms and legs were flailing around wildly as he dropped to the ground. His body came down with a crashing thud. The bike landed on its wheels and bounced out of the way. The Ringers could hear all the air crush out of him with a loud *oof.* As the guys ran over, Eric curled into a ball.

They could tell right away that Eric was OK. They had all had falls like that in the Pits. Willy was smiling as he helped Jim get Eric to his feet. Eric was weak from a lack of air and reached both arms out for support.

And then Willy saw it. He could tell that Sam saw it too, because they both gasped and took a step back.

"Gross!" Sam said softly.

Willy said nothing.

Eric's hand wasn't normal. It wasn't even the right color. He had only three fingers—short, little fingers that all pointed in different directions. Willy couldn't tell if they had fingernails. His skin was a kind of lifeless gray color. Eric was still out of breath as he tried to stand weakly, and as Willy stepped away, he let Eric fall over. Jim tried harder to help him up. "Will you guys give me a hand?" Jim said with frustration, not really looking at them. "He needs to walk it off."

Willy and Sam looked at each other.

29

CHOICE ➡

If Willy and Sam help, turn to page 61.
If they don't, turn to page 111.

Sam said nothing. Willy got irritated. "Sam!" he blurted out, at a loss for what else to say. He and Sam caught up to Jim and Eric before they even got back to the bikes. Willy grabbed Jim by the arm and said, "Wait a minute! This is totally stupid. We're not all gonna freak out just because of Sam's big mouth."

Jim and Eric turned and looked angrily at Sam.

Sam turned away as he spoke: "That was dumb," he admitted. "I didn't mean to bum out on your hand. It just took me off guard." He turned around and looked at Eric's hand stuffed in his pocket. "What happened? Was it some accident?"

"No. I've always been this way." He pulled out his hand and held it up to see. Willy could see a little anger in Eric's eyes as he told them about it, about growing up looking weird and always having to hide his faults. Eric couldn't play many of the sports that the other guys liked. He could never take a gym class, and he often felt left out. It didn't seem fair that people would reject him for his hand. . . . But then, that's what Sam had done just a few minutes before. *It's hard not to,* they thought as Eric spoke. Still, Sam's apology spared them from a lot of grief that day.

A lot of grief.

THE END

If you haven't read about some of the grief they dodged, turn to page 97 and make different choices along the way.

Or, turn to page 141.

Head for the bikes!" Willy yelled as they ran from the cave. All three stayed together as they crossed the clearing at top speed.

The old man and the cop watched them for a second in disbelief, then started yelling and chasing after them. Willy could see over his shoulder as he ran that the cop had left the old man behind and was quickly overtaking them. "Run! Run! Run!" he yelled.

They hit the brush where they had left Eric, but Eric was nowhere to be seen. Without slowing down to look, all three burst through the bushes and headed straight for the Sinks. The branches tore and pulled at them as they crashed through. And then they were in the light again. They rounded the edge of the Sink and ran toward their bikes as fast as they could. They could hear the cop ripping through the trees right behind them.

Suddenly Willy heard a man scream.

He looked over his shoulder just in time to see the cop flying through the air and land headlong in the Sink. Eric came out of the bushes just where they had all gone into the woods. He climbed out of some low bushes and started running after them. "Go! Go!" he was yelling. They did.

As the cop was splashing to shore and the old man was just now coming through the bushes, the Ringers and

Eric were already mounted on their bikes and pedaling up the rise out of the Sinks. They had grabbed all their stuff and just carried it out as they rode. About a half a mile down the road, they stopped just long enough to arrange their stuff so they could pedal harder.

"We have to get off the road!" said Sam.

"One is in a car and the other is on a street bike, so we can hide on the run better going through the fields all the way back to town," said Willy.

"Let's meet at the Freeze as soon as we get there," Jim added.

"And where were you?" Willy screeched at Eric.

"*I* whistled. I was there, but you guys didn't hear me. So I watched and figured you guys would eventually try to escape."

Without a word, Willy turned and rode off between the trees into the woods. The others followed. It was slow going, but soon they were far from the road. And then, about halfway home, as they were coming out of the fields into a housing development, they all saw the Vipers' pickup truck slowly cruising one of the streets. They were looking for someone.

As they watched the pickup drive slowly by, they put the rest of their clothes on and watched anxiously, catching their breath.

"Well," said Eric, "you guys sure know how to have fun!"

"Yeah," Sam said sarcastically, "this is pretty much a normal Friday night, wouldn't you say, Jim?"

Jim nodded. "Yeah."

Willy pushed his bike and rode into the open. The Vipers seemed to have cleared out, so it was time to head into town. This was the part of the trip that Willy was not looking forward to. After about two blocks he stopped and waited for the other guys.

"Look," he said, "everyone is looking for four guys in bathing suits on bikes, right? So what we need to do is split up and get to the Freeze. Once we're there we can hide out. Jim, you and Eric go first, and try to look casual. After a while Sam and I will leave and take a different route. Maybe that'll throw them off." They all took off without another word. Sam and Willy stood by a telephone pole and waited.

"Willy," said Sam with some concern in his voice, "what do you think is going on? Who were those guys?"

"I've been thinking about that the whole way home, and I don't know. Maybe Mr. Whitehead can help us when we get back."

With that they left. Around every corner they expected to see an old man or a cop on a bike or the Vipers, but they didn't. When they finally got back to Millersburg, Willy sighed with relief and thanked God as they pulled up to the Freeze and parked their bikes around back. Sam and Willy came in the back entrance and took a seat at the counter.

Betty came over and looked at them. "You two look like you've been overlicked by a cat," she said with a laugh.

Sam winced.

"What can I get you boys?"

"Water!" Willy and Sam both said at the same time. They gulped down a whole glass each.

Finally Eric and Jim came in. They all sat together. After Eric and Jim had downed several glasses of water, they talked about what to do next.

"I think we're safe," Willy said. "Everything happened out at the Sinks, which is two light years away. I think if we stay away from there long enough, this whole thing will blow over."

"That's a good point," said Sam.

"We should tell somebody," Jim protested. "What if it *doesn't* blow over? What if we need for somebody to know?"

"That's also a good point," said Sam.

They sat in their booth for a while and thought about it, each with his own thoughts. "We could tell Zeke," Willy offered. They all instantly agreed. Zeke would know what to do next, if nothing else.

"Or we could tell my grandfather," Jim suggested. They all agreed to that, too, but with more hesitation. Mr. Whitehead was a pastor and a retired missionary. What if he told them the right thing to do and they didn't like it? They would almost have to do it anyway. It would be safer to tell Zeke. He loved God as Mr. Whitehead did, and they admired him for it, but he was still only eighteen. He didn't carry that aura of automatic authority that older Christians like Mr. Whitehead did.

Finally Willy decided he would tell his brother all about it that night. "Give me your hands," he said. "This is our secret pact. Everything we saw today is our secret. No one can know . . . except the Ringers . . . and Zeke . . . and Mr. Whitehead." They shook on it and it was a done deal.

36

As they walked out of the Freeze, it was almost dark. "Well," said Willy, "the weekend is here." Then he turned to Eric and the guys and said, "Come to my place and sleep over. The weekend is only just beginning!" Surely more was ahead.

THE END

What was the old man hiding? Are the police in on it? To find out more, go back to page 1 and make different choices along the way.

Or, turn to page 141.

Last one in is a rotten tamale!" Willy suddenly shouted. He turned and made a run for the other Sink. The other guys came crashing along after Willy, but his lead was too great. He passed the land-bridge that divided the two lakes and headed for the stand of trees along the far edge of the Sink.

A rope hung from a tree there, and Willy knew that if he got there first, he would be in control of it. And if he were in control, he could make the other guys beg to use it. He leapt through the air as he rounded the edge of the Sink and grabbed the rope in midair. His feet splashed across the surface of the water as the tree bent with his weight. He parked himself on the rope, swinging slowly back and forth as the other guys came up and stood on the bank to watch. "It's my rope now!"

The other guys all sprang into the water and headed straight for Willy. He knew what they were up to. They were going to overthrow him. It was like a water version of King of the Hill that they always played at the rope. But Willy knew who would come out on top. The guys grabbed Willy's legs, and the weight of three of them pulled Willy off without much effort. After several kings of the rope, the game grew old and the guys paddled off in different directions to explore various parts of the Sink. There was always cool stuff to find there.

38

Eric paired off with Willy, and they worked their way down past the far corner of the Sink and up a small stream in the brush. They were on the trail of some lizards they saw when they heard voices. Immediately they crouched down and became silent. Up ahead they could hear several people talking. They crept closer. It was the Vipers, four of them. Willy grabbed Eric's arm and told him to keep quiet.

The Vipers were gathered around this old man. The man had gray hair and striking blue eyes that Willy could see all the way across the clearing. The old man was sitting on a big rock with a box between his feet. A few feet farther away stood an old pickup truck, with the Vipers' symbol on the bumper. Next to the truck was an old sky-blue car from the fifties or sixties. The old man and the Vipers were talking loudly, but Eric and Willy couldn't really make out their words. The old man was giving things to the Vipers, and the Vipers were giving money to the old man.

They backed out of their hiding spot and headed back toward the Sink. As they came out near the water, they waved for the other guys to come over.

"We got problems," Willy said in a hushed voice. "Back there in a clearing we saw some of the Vipers. They were doing some kind of drug deal or something with an old guy."

"How do you know that?" Jim asked.

"We don't, really," answered Eric. "But they were doing something with packages and money. *You* figure it out."

As they were there talking about what they should do, the Vipers' truck came ripping out of the woods from back where Willy had seen them. All four of the Vipers were in the truck. Willy and the guys crouched down and watched them drive off.

"That looked like all of them," Eric said.

"No," said Willy, "the old man is still back there. He had an old blue car."

"We should get out of here," said Jim.

"I say we check this out," said Sam.

CHOICE

If they decide to check out the old man, turn to page 84.

If they decide to get out of there, turn to page 122.

Don't worry so much about doing time," Willy said. "Let's get some food and do it. I don't have anything planned until church Sunday morning."

"Cool," said Sam, looking over Willy's shoulder at the other guys. Well?"

Jim looked at the ground for a second as Eric stared into space. It was obvious that Eric would do whatever they all decided to do. "OK," Jim finally said. "I'll ask my grandparents and see if we can stay overnight at the church in case things don't work out at the Sinks."

"Great! OK, then, this is the plan." They all gathered around Willy. "There are blankets already stored up at the Sink fort, and we won't be too cold anyway. All we need is to get some food and get out of here."

"And the green light from headquarters," added Sam.

"Of course."

They all jumped on their bikes. Eric got unsteadily on the back of Jim's. Willy noticed he kept one of his hands in his pocket as he unsteadily climbed on Jim's bike and almost knocked them both over. Sam pointed and laughed. "Where's your bike?" Willy said.

Without looking Willy in the eye, Eric said, "I didn't bring a bike with me on the bus."

"Oh yeah," said Willy. "Everybody go home and get permission and stuff, and we'll all meet back here in fifteen minutes." They all set off. Willy went home and, after getting permission from headquarters (Mom), grabbed a bunch of hot dogs out of the freezer. He was in and out of the apartment in about three seconds and on his way back to the Common. Sam was already there when he pulled up.

"What do you think of this Eric guy?" Sam said.

"I don't know," Willy answered thoughtfully. "He is from Emeryville, but I don't want to judge him too quickly. It's hard to think something about a guy who doesn't say anything and who never looks you in the eye."

"Well," said Sam, sitting in the grass, "he seems weird to me. It's like he tries to be nowhere while he's standing right here. They breed strange beings over there in Emeryville. I heard about this one kid—"

Just then Jim and Eric pulled up on separate bikes. Jim had his bike, but Eric was riding an old bike with fat tires and a black and white saddle seat that looked as if it pinched and bit every time you sat on it. The old bike rattled and clanked loudly as Eric followed Jim across the grass on the Common. Sam and Willy smiled as they pulled up.

"I thought you said you left your bike at home," Willy laughed as they pulled to a stop.

"This isn't my bike," Eric said with disgust. "This was Jim's idea."

"There's no way I could carry him all the way out to the Sinks on the back of my bike. I'd have to crash out as soon as we got there. This is an old bike from my garage. I think it was my grandfather's from waaaayy back in the fifties."

"You mean back in the *twenties*," Sam laughed.

"Whatever," said Willy. "Let's get going."

They mounted up and started out of town—Willy, then Sam, then Jim, and then Eric, clattering in the rear. They rode out of town, south, out into the country. They kept to the side of the road as they went up and down the slightly rising and falling hills. The woods along the road thickened as they went farther and farther. As they rode, Willy would occasionally turn and glance at Eric at the end of the line. Eric rode with two hands on the handlebars, but whenever Willy looked back, Eric would switch to using only one hand, stuffing his right hand in his pocket.

Finally, they rounded a bend and came upon the Sinks. They pulled to a stop and looked out over the water. Below them, not too far down, stood the two square lakes that made up "the Sinks." That's just what they looked like—two square sinks set in a green, mossy countertop. The guys had built a secret fort up above them, on the top of a rise that overlooked the Sinks on one side and the rolling fields and forests on the other.

"Well, Eric," Willy said, "welcome to the Sinks!"

"Cool."

"I say we go for a swim," said Willy.

Sam looked over at Willy and nodded agreement.

"I say we set up camp," said Jim, dropping his knapsack to the ground. Everybody turned and looked at him. "You know, stash the food . . . and maybe eat some too."

CHOICE ⟹

If they decide to swim, turn to page 97.

If they decide to set up camp, turn to page 70.

Jim looked around, then looked quickly behind him. Up in the factory, they could hear the other guys yelling to each other from somewhere inside. After a minute or two, Jim shook his head and said, "I shouldn't say anything because I promised. But you won't tell anyone."

Willy smiled. "What's so secret?"

"I know what Eric hides in his pocket and why he's so quiet."

"Does it have anything to do with dead hamsters?"

Jim half smiled and half frowned. "What?"

"Never mind. What's the deal with Eric?"

"I followed him in gym class one day and saw him back with the nurse," Jim whispered. "She was doing something to his hand, so I got closer so I could see. I walked into the office like I had a bellyache, and she was holding his hand out. It was not normal."

Willy's eyes widened a little. "What do you mean 'not normal'?"

Jim looked away as he spoke. "He only has three fingers on his hand, and they're all gray-colored. It was pretty gross."

"What did the nurse and Eric do when you came in?"

"The nurse didn't do anything, but Eric got mad. He started yelling at me. I spent the whole class in the nurse's office until we got to be friends."

"Did he have his hand out the whole time?"

"Not at first, but he got used to it. He's really not a bad guy. We were actually cracking jokes."

"Wow," Willy said to himself softly. He had never met a person like that before. Maybe that was why Eric was so quiet; he was embarrassed. All of a sudden he understood why Eric acted so creepy. Eric was different. "I never met somebody like that before," he said.

"It's really nothing," Jim said. "After a while you don't think about it."

"Then why is Eric so weird about it?"

"He told me he's afraid of being in a new school and having people make fun of him. It's happened before." Jim grabbed Willy's arm and looked him in the eye. "The only reason I told you is that I know you won't make a big deal out of it. You know what it's like to be different. But I know how uncomfortable it makes Eric, so don't say anything about it, OK?"

"OK."

The two started walking together toward the factory. They climbed in through half a door that was left on the back and called to the others. After a minute, Eric and Sam came running down from a flight of stairs above. The four stood in the back hall. Eric and Sam were out of breath, and Eric still had his hand stuffed down his pocket. Willy couldn't help staring. They all stepped back out into the yard to talk where the air was cooler.

"This place seems pretty cool," Eric said. "I'd love to explore the rest of it before we go back down to the motocross."

46

"Sure. Sure," said Willy, and he motioned for Jim and Eric to go ahead. Then he turned to talk with Sam.

If Willy tells Sam, turn to page 100.

If Willy keeps the secret, turn to page 12.

The overwhelming vote went for forgetting about the old-man incident.

"OK, OK." Willy gave in.

Boy, was *that* a mistake!

THE END

Are you kidding? *Forget about it?* Only if your mom's calling you for dinner! Otherwise, turn to page 1, make different choices along the way, and see what else lies in store for the Ringers and their mystery man with the box.

OK," Willy whispered, "then let's sneak off down the side of the hill. We'll circle away from the way we came and cut back through the fort on the top of the hill. It's shorter and there's more cover that way."

They came out of the cave and crawled along the hill to the left. They all moved as slowly and silently as cats. It was about fifteen yards until they would hit a small grove of trees that stretched all the way up the hill to the back of their fort. The going was slow, but after about ten minutes, they were up to the trees. One by one they got to the trees and stood up, each waiting for the one behind him to get there before heading up the hill. They were halfway up the hill when they heard a motorcycle down below. They all stopped and looked back down to see what was going on.

It was a motorcycle cop. He got off his bike and shook the man's hand, and the two stood talking for several minutes.

"Do you think that's a bad cop?" Sam said. "That old guy seemed pretty criminal if he's hanging out with the Vipers. Maybe the cop's on the take?"

"Shhh," said Willy. "Maybe we can hear them."

After a few more minutes, they both went into the cave. "Wow," said Jim, "if we were still in there we'd be dead meat by now."

"Or live meat *becoming* dead," suggested Sam.

The two men were in the cave for about fifteen minutes, which seemed like forever to the guys. The guys were just getting ready to leave when Jim saw Eric stick his head out of the clearing. An electric shock went through Willy. He grabbed Sam's arm and pointed at Eric without saying a word.

As the guys watched, Eric edged closer and closer to the cave mouth. Sam came out of the trees a little and started frantically waving his arms, but Eric wouldn't look up. He was too engrossed in sneaking up and looking in the cave.

Finally Willy couldn't stand it anymore. He came out of the trees and whistled loudly.

Eric stood bolt upright and looked up at the trees. Suddenly a horrified look came across his face and he turned to run, but it was too late. The cop and the old man were out of the cave and on top of him in a flash. Sam and Willy got back down and watched from the trees. Their hearts sank as they watched the men lead Eric across the clearing and into the back of the car. The two men stood talking for a second. Then the old man got in his car and the cop climbed on his motorcycle, and they started to leave.

"Come on!" Willy yelled, "we have to follow them!" They all went ripping over the top of the hill, through the fort area and down to the spot where they had left their bikes. But it took too long to get over the hill, and by the time they were on their bikes, the car and the cop were gone.

Willy felt like he was going to throw up. He had asked

Eric to be the lookout, and now Eric was a hostage. Just then, a flash of chrome caught his eye.

Willy looked over toward the Dead Sink and saw the back end of his brother's car, the "Batmobile." He raced over screaming, "Zeke! Zeke!"

Zeke slowed and rolled down his window. "I've been looking for you. Mom told me . . ." Willy couldn't hold it in any longer.

"Zeke! Eric just got kidnapped!" Suddenly they were all yelling at once. "Eric got taken away by a policeman and an old guy who deals drugs to the Vipers just now! We think the police are in on it. We have to find him."

Zeke shook his head and said, "What? Slow down, one at a time." Willy, Sam, and Jim told him everything that had happened over the last half an hour. Zeke immediately threw all the bikes (including Eric's) into the huge trunk of his car and tied down the lid with some clothesline. They all piled in and started for town.

"The first thing we have to do is call the police," said Zeke.

"No, no," Willy said insistently, "one of them *was* the police!"

"Did it ever occur to you that maybe they were *both* the police?"

It hadn't.

"Did you junior detectives happen to get a license plate number?"

"Yeah!" said Jim. "I looked, but I forgot. It was *SC* something. Virginia."

"Well," said Zeke, "we have two options: we can head

straight for the police, which is what I think we should do; or we can look around for ourselves."

If they scout around on their own, turn to page 108.

If they call the police, turn to page 92.

The next words that came out of Willy's mouth surprised even him. "You guys aren't welcome here. You can go do your drugs somewhere else."

The Vipers were not amused. They started walking slowly toward Willy. "What, puke?"

Willy swallowed hard. "What do you guys want with this place anyway? You already control the best spots in town."

The bigger guy took a step closer toward Willy as he spoke. "Territory is everything, puke. Maybe we just might start hanging out down here. From now on this is our place." He grabbed Willy by the collar and drew back his fist. As Willy got ready to be hit and throw his own punch, he thought he heard someone laugh behind the guy grabbing him, but the Viper never saw what hit him. Suddenly his face was surprised and angry and in pain all at once. His grip on Willy's collar was loosened instantly as he fell with a crash on his back. There, standing over him, was Eric.

"I wouldn't get back up," Eric said coolly. But the Viper did. They squared off and Willy stepped back in amazement. All the guys made a circle around the two.

"You're going to wish you were never born, puke!" the Viper spit out at Eric.

"I don't think so," said Eric with a smile.

As the Vipers all cheered and hooted, the two fighters circled, looking for the best way to take the other down. Finally the Viper lunged with a right to Eric's face. But Eric leaned back and let the punch fly harmlessly past his head. As the big Viper passed, Eric reached under his arm and pivoted his body. He tossed the big boy into a railing by the stairs, and the gang member just slouched onto the floor. "Get up! Get up!" the other Vipers shrieked at their fallen man.

He finally did. He circled around and came at Eric full speed, but Eric let him pass and tripped him as he went by. The big Viper went reeling and slammed into a wall. As he slid to the floor, a mist of fine dust fell from the ceiling on his body. He was down and out.

The two that were still in good shape helped the thrashed Viper to his feet. "Don't think you're out of this yet, pukes," the big Viper said groggily. "We can find you." They retreated down the stairs.

Sam came over and patted Eric on the back. "That was totally killer! You could have murdered those guys all by yourself!"

"Where did you learn to do that?" asked Willy in amazement. "I never thought you could fight."

"I learned to take care of myself a long time ago." He held up his hand for the guys to see. It was small—only three fingers that were curled into a fist. The skin was a dull gray.

"Cool," said Sam.

"I told him you guys knew and were talking about him when you were downstairs," said Jim. "Just as well."

"Yeah, thanks man," Willy said, stretching out his hand to shake. Eric smiled and put his small hand right in Willy's. Willy was a little shocked at first, that he had just stuck out his hand and Eric shook it, but Eric's small hand felt just like a normal hand, except that it was smaller and the pressure from his squeeze was in different places than he was used to. "I think I owe you one."

"Well," said Eric, "I know a way you could make it up."

"What's that?"

"Give me another chance on the motocross."

"No problem!" Willy said.

They all started down to the Pits. They were careful on their way out to look for Vipers, but they seemed to have cleared out. As they crossed the Pits, they could see police patrolling the neighborhood. They knew that the Vipers would be nowhere nearby.

THE END

There are more adventures to come. Turn back to page 1 and make different choices along the way.

Or, turn to page 141.

Suddenly Willy felt a strong urge to get to know Eric better. The timing seemed pretty good, too. Sam was out on the trail, Jim was always ready to talk, and if it started to go bad he was next on the motocross and could excuse himself and regroup.

Willy started in, "You know Jim, that's not a bad idea about having Eric come over and see the church and maybe come to a service."

Jim thought about it a second and then said, "Yeah, he could meet all the guys—Chris and Pete will be back from the science competition by Sunday." He turned to Eric and said, "You'd like Chris and Pete."

Eric didn't say anything at first; he just listened with interest. Jim and Willy told him about the service and what usually happened there. "I'd have to ask my mom if it would be OK," he finally said. "I have to tell you, the last church I went to was pretty boring. This one sounds like it might be better, though."

"You can sleep over at my house this whole weekend," Jim said. Just then, Sam pulled up in a cloud of dust and screamed a kind of war cry. Apparently he was pleased with his run.

"Hey Sam!" Willy called him over. "Eric's going to church with us on Sunday!"

"Cool. Maybe he could become one of the Ringers!"

56

Eric smiled. It had been a long time since a group of kids his age actually wanted to include him in *anything*. He decided he was going to like this "gang" a lot better than the ones in Emeryville.

THE END

Eric, Jim, Willy, and Sam go through a number of adventures together. To find out more about an old man, a mystery box, and the police, go back to page 5 and make different choices along the way.

Or, turn to page 141.

Willy looked around the group. All the guys looked at him expectantly, waiting for him to decide what to vote. His first impulse was to get mad, but he fought it.

"Well?" Sam said.

"OK," Willy said, a smile breaking on his face. "We have the whole weekend. Maybe we can pull an all-nighter later on or something. Let's go look for some crockamonkies."

They all pulled their bikes up and began to mount them. "Wait a minute," Sam said. "There are four of us and only three bikes." He looked hard at Eric and said, "Don't they have bikes in Emeryville?"

"Yeah," Eric said softly, "I have a bike, but I didn't bring it with me on the bus. I haven't been home today."

"Don't worry about it, Eric," Jim said. "You can ride with me. Climb on." Eric climbed awkwardly onto Jim's seat, never pulling his right hand out of his worn jacket pocket. Willy and Sam watched as the two rode wobbly off down the street, Jim standing on his pedals.

"I don't know about this Eric guy," said Willy.

"He definitely seems weird," said Sam, pulling the red backpack on as he spoke. "He hasn't taken his hand out of his pocket since I met him an hour ago. It's like he's hiding something down there, like a gun or something."

Sam started to push off his bike and ride away. "Maybe he has a claw," he laughed over his shoulder. "Maybe he's one of the mutants that live in the Pits, and he's just luring us down there so they can eat us aliiiiive!"

Willy shook his head as he caught up with Sam. "I think you've been watching too much TV," he laughed.

They caught up with Jim and Eric quickly. After a few blocks, a low, black Chrysler pulled alongside the three bikes. It was Zeke. "What you guys doing?"

Willy cruised to a stop and the other guys followed his lead. "We're going down to the Pits to motocross. Do you want to meet us down there?"

Zeke laughed and shook his head. "Yeah, right," he said. "You just watch out. I saw Grossman and some of his Viper idiots headed this way. Just watch out for them." Bill Grossman was a leader of the Vipers gang that hung around the suburbs of D.C. Normally they didn't show up in quaint, historic Millersburg, but that didn't mean they *never* showed up.

Zeke revved his car a little. Then the car moved away, smooth and slow. Willy hated when Zeke treated him like a kid, but he knew that he wouldn't see much of him as soon as college started, so he would take what he could get.

"Who was that?" Eric asked.

"That was my too-cool brother, Zeke," Willy said. The four cruised down Elm Street and across town toward the factory. They rode past the old factory and swooped into the field behind. The Ringers each fishtailed to a stop in his own turn and looked back, triumphantly waiting to watch the others arrive. Jim and Eric came last, slowly coasting to a stop. Jim slammed on his brake at the last second and skidded a few feeble inches. Everyone laughed.

In front of them stood the Pits—a huge lot with great piles of dirt overgrown with weeds. Sticking out from the weeds were odd handles and angled machinery that looked like they had been there for a hundred years and were being reclaimed by the land. It was quiet, except for the loud whining noise made by a billion insects.

"So Eric," Sam said too loudly, throwing the backpack over in the bushes by the gate as he spoke. "You ever been here before?"

Eric looked confused. "No. Of course not."

Willy stepped over and slapped Eric on the shoulder and motioned for him to follow. Eric stiffened and followed reluctantly. "Don't worry, Eric. This place is cool."

"What *is* this place?" Eric said uneasily.

"This place is *ours*," said Willy with authority. "Mr. Whitehead, a friend of ours from church, told me that the Pits were really a staging area for the factory when they made furniture here."

They walked along together, Willy pushing his bike with one hand and waving bugs away with the other as he spoke. Eric listened closely, his head down, both hands thrust into his pockets. "The dirt was piled here by the factory owners when they dug out the basement," Willy continued. "We'll go check that out later. They used to store trucks and worn-out equipment here. And the place is ours. We made a motocross here."

"Enough talk already," Sam said with annoyance. "You're as bad as a couple of yapping girls." He squirmed past them and jumped on his bike. "This is how it's done."

60

As the others watched, Sam pedaled around the corner of a machine-bush and disappeared. After a few seconds he appeared again, flying from the top of a mound of dirt. As he flew through the air he turned his front wheel to the left and screamed, just like a racer. Sam came to a crash landing at the foot of the hill and nearly lost control of his bike before straightening out and riding back to the other guys. He was out of breath as he pulled up.

"Killer!" Willy said. "I'm next!"

"Wait," Sam said, grabbing his arm and not taking his eyes off Eric. "I think we should see Eric do it." Eric stepped back, pulling his arms tightly into his sides and shoving his hands further into his pockets.

Eric looked back and forth nervously from Sam's bike to Sam's smiling face.

If they make Eric ride, turn to page 27.

If they let Eric watch, turn to page 116.

Willy and Sam both stepped over and helped Jim get Eric back on his feet. Eric tried to stick his right hand back in his pocket, but the pocket was turned inside out, and he couldn't. He pushed and pushed the shriveled hand into the gray folds of the pocket, but it wouldn't go in. The three Ringers stood entranced. Finally Eric stopped trying and let his arm hang limp at his side.

"What happened to you?" Sam asked a little breathlessly.

"Wow," Willy said out loud.

Eric began to sniffle as he looked away toward the factory.

"Hey, man," Jim said, "it's OK. Like I told you, you're among friends here." Jim punched Eric on the shoulder as friends do. "Why don't you tell them. They're cool."

Eric looked back. Willy was surprised to see that his eyes were dry. Eric seemed like the crying type when they first met. But there was a different look in his eyes now; a look of determination. "You can tell us, man," Willy said.

Eric held up his hand. "This is my hand," he said. "Other guys have called it all kinds of names, but all it is is my hand." He wiggled the little gray fingers without fingernails, and Willy felt a chill go down his spine.

"What happened?" asked Sam.

Eric sighed and smiled at Sam. "Nothing happened to

it. I was born like this. My doctor said I had a virus when I was in my mom and almost died, but somehow I survived."

"In your mother's womb I knew you," Jim said softly.

Eric turned and looked surprised at him. "What?"

"That's what God says in the Bible." Jim smiled as he spoke. "From the very beginning to the very end, God knows you and protects you—Jeremiah 1:5."

"That's why you're here now," said Willy.

Eric laughed and worked his hand into his pocket. "You guys sound like you go to church. We don't go." He started to walk back to the other bikes by the gate. "Ever since my parents got divorced, we haven't gone to any of that stuff. My dad says that all religions are the same, anyway."

Jim laughed. "That's like saying all cars are the same, or all people are the same."

"Or all *hands!*" Sam added in a flash of brilliance.

Eric nodded as if to say, "Good point." Then he continued: "Well, I'm not too sure how much God knows or cares about me right now."

"You're welcome to go with us to church and find out," Sam said. "We even have a club down at the church. I mean down at Mr. Whitehead's church. We're the ringers there."

"The what?"

"The ringers," Willy chimed in. "We ring the bell."

"Oh."

"It also means that we try to be like Jesus," Jim said boldly. " 'Ringer' means a person who acts like someone else, and we try to be like Jesus."

"Doesn't always work, though," Sam admitted, "as you probably can tell."

"Not everybody thinks it's cool," Willy added.

"So we stick together," said Jim. "And we all go to Capitol Community Church—Mr. Whitehead's church."

Eric seemed impressed. "Hmm. I'd like to go to church again."

"Then consider this an official invite," Willy said with a bow.

"All right."

The four guys pushed their bikes up toward the head of the trails and then spent five minutes figuring out the order they would ride. First Sam would go; he'd set the pace. Then it would be Willy's turn, then Eric's, then Jim's.

Willy watched Eric closely; he decided he wanted to ask Eric to hang out with them more often. He knew that if Chris were there, he would probably do something like that—maybe even ask Eric to be a Ringer, eventually. Willy didn't really know what the Holy Spirit wanted for him, really, *actually*. Willy had to pray about it first and trust that God was moving him to do the right thing.

When Sam was out on his ride, Willy had the chance to talk to Eric. But he was so new and different that Willy didn't know what to say—or even whether he wanted to say anything.

64

CHOICE ➡

If Willy talks to Eric, turn to page 55.
If Willy doesn't, turn to page 16.

"OK," said Willy, "we'll leave the box hidden over there with the knapsack by the front gate." The four stashed the box and snuck over to the entrance of the factory. As they climbed the old rickety stairs, they told Eric about the time they spied on a man and a little boy they all thought was a kidnapped kid, but who turned out to be just some people staying in the old house. Once up in a room on the third floor, they looked down at the house.

"Jim," Willy whispered, "did you see where he went in?"

"No. He just went in and that was all."

They all crouched by the window and looked down for what seemed like forever. The beat-up old house looked as it always did—chipped paint, overgrown grass, drawn shades, and a broken-down car on the front lawn. "People at school say they sell drugs in that house," said Sam.

"Not all houses like that are full of drugs," said Eric. All the guys turned and looked at him. Eric turned red and looked away. "We have a lot of those houses over in Emeryville. My house looks like that."

The guys didn't know what to say.

Just then the old man came out the front door. He was hunched over and seemed to be carrying something under his arm. He came down the steps, walked around the wrecked car, and moved quickly up the street back toward the Pits. The guys moved silently out of their lookout room and down the hall to watch him from another window. From there they could see his white hair move through the hills and back toward the woods. He disappeared in the trees.

"If he's looking for his loot, he's in for a big surprise," Willy whispered with a small laugh. After about five minutes, the old man emerged and looked up at the factory. It seemed as if he looked right up at the window they were looking out. Then he moved slowly through the Pits, working his way through the hills toward the factory—as if he had heard what Willy had said and was on his way to make him take it back.

"Let's get out of here!" said Jim.

All the guys jumped up and started to run for the door, not caring how much noise they were making. As they ran down the stairs, Sam kept saying, "What about the bikes? What about the bikes?" But they didn't head in the direction that they had come in. They ran through the factory away from the Pits, toward the exit at the other end.

Willy stopped and let the others pass. "We can get the stuff later. If he catches us in here we're dead meat."

Just as they reached the door, a crash from deep inside the factory startled them. "It sounds like he's pushing down the walls!" said Eric.

Racing out to the opposite side of the factory, the four came to stop at the end of the small fenced parking lot that stood cracked and abandoned on the other side of the factory. As they stood panting, the door burst open and the old man stepped out onto the deck. He held a long pipe in his hands. "Where is it, you punks?" he boomed.

The man started to come down the steps. He swung the pipe and smashed out a window behind him as he came.

All four guys started shaking with fear. The man stood between them and the only way out of the parking lot. "God, help us," Jim said. "Please help us!"

Willy instinctively picked up a rock. "It's over by our stuff! On the other side of the factory! Over by the gate! We didn't touch anything. It's all there!" The idea of being hit by that pipe had him so scared that his voice fluttered and squeaked as he yelled.

The man stopped at the bottom of the stairs, glared, climbed back up the stairs, and disappeared into the building. The four guys looked at each other in relief.

"It worked! Thank you, Lord!" squealed Jim.

"He's probably going to smash our bikes!" said Sam.

Just then a van pulled into the parking lot. Mr. Whitehead was driving, with Mrs. Whitehead in the passenger seat. The van pulled up to them and Mr. Whitehead looked out. "Aren't you guys coming down to the church? You're late for our barbecue!"

They had completely forgotten.

"Hi, Eric!" said Mrs. Whitehead.

Eric smiled wide and waved back with his deformed hand. "Hey Mrs. W!"

Sam and Willy suddenly erupted all at once: "There was a guy in the factory who almost beat our heads in. . . ."

"A guy tried to kill us, we have his box of stolen stuff. . . ."

"You just scared off a guy that was gonna kill us. . . ."

Mr. and Mrs. Whitehead eventually got most of the

details of what actually happened, but they didn't seem too alarmed. "If you guys had been down at the church for the barbecue where you were supposed to be, you wouldn't be having this little emergency, now would you?"

"Where are your bikes?" Mr. Whitehead continued. "I saw you all ride out of town over an hour ago."

"They're on the other side," said Willy excitedly. "We have to go get them!" They all climbed into the van and drove around the building. "He probably smashed them all to pieces," announced Sam matter-of-factly as they pulled up to the other side. But the bikes were where they left them, lying undamaged. The old man and the box were gone.

The guys loaded the bikes into the van, and Mr. Whitehead drove them all back to the church. Eric stayed for the barbecue.

"You know, someday we're going to have to have a rematch back at the motocross. You didn't get another chance to ride," Willy said to Eric through a chicken leg. Over the last several hours, and after getting to know Eric a little, neither Willy nor Sam seemed to notice, or care, that Eric had a deformed hand.

Eric nodded. "Sounds cool. Only this time I'll show you some moves of my own."

"What moves?" queried Sam.

"You'll see," said Eric, winking.

69

THE END

What moves? And who is that crazy man? To find out more, turn to page 1 and make different choices along the way.

Willy stood there thinking for a second. Then he answered, "OK, that's not a bad idea. You know how I feel about food." They pedaled down the slope and across the narrow land-bridge that separated the two lakes. Toward the end they all leaned into their riding and sped up to climb the hill that led up to their fort. But it didn't really matter. All the pedaling in the world couldn't help them make it to the top. So about halfway they had to get off their bikes, lay them down, shoulder their packs, and climb the rest of the way by foot.

Near the top they could hear voices. They motioned each other to stop and crouch down.

"There's someone up there," Willy whispered. They advanced slowly toward the fort. Through the bushes they could see who was there. It was Bill Grossman, the leader of a D.C. gang, and three of his gang friends. Willy, Sam, Jim, and Eric lay under some bushes and watched to see what they were doing. Bill was watching as the other three guys finished kicking down the wooden lean-to the Ringers had built as their fort. They were all bigger and older than the Ringers. They wore their colors, black jeans, and boots with chains across the heels. They smoked cigarettes and swore and laughed as they pulled the blankets out of their bags and began tearing them. One of the Vipers pulled out a knife and began slicing up one of the blankets. It was the gray wool blanket Willy's parents had given him for camping out.

They laughed as they destroyed the place. Willy started to rise, getting ready to charge into the camp, but Jim grabbed his shoulder and pulled him down.

"Are you insane?" Jim whispered.

Willy watched, his face showing anger. "If my brother Zeke were here he would help. We could get them." He looked over at Eric, who was watching him. Part of him wanted to get those guys to show Eric that he wasn't a wimp. But he also knew Jim was right. Jim was always so cool and levelheaded.

"There's nothing we can do," Sam said. "They were here before we could stop them—"

"Wait a minute," Grossman said holding up his arm. The other Vipers stopped what they were doing and looked around. Grossman walked slowly across the clearing and stopped just a few feet above where the guys were hiding. He looked down into the Sinks. The Ringers quietly looked over their shoulders, down below. Willy hoped it was Zeke pulling in for a swim. Sometimes he liked to come up here too.

Down below, an old blue car splashed with gray mud pulled in slowly and paused by the first turn around the water. A big old man with gray hair stepped out and looked around. Grossman whistled a horrendously loud whistle and the old man nodded and got back in his car and drove slowly around the bend out of sight.

"Hey, you guys," Grossman called, "come 'ere." The other Vipers came over and they all stood right over the

Ringers. "The old coot just drove in down there," Grossman said with a sneer. "We're finished here. Let's go see how much the old man will give us and if he has anything for us to do." The Vipers all turned and walked away across the camp and headed into the woods at the back and disappeared.

After a few seconds the guys climbed out of the brush and looked around at the damage. The lean-to was a total loss. The Vipers had broken every stick into a twig, leaving nothing to be salvaged. Willy and Sam gathered all of the wood into a pile. Eric just stood by and watched as the guys went through the debris and found their stuff: a torn blanket, smashed glasses, and squashed pots. After about ten minutes of silent scavenging, they had assessed the damage: everything was wrecked except one small pot and a hot dog skewer.

Down below they could hear an engine roar to life, a souped-up engine that banged and fired. They walked to the same point the Vipers had stood and looked down. A beat-up pickup rattled past the water—two Vipers in the front, two in back with their shirts off.

Sam looked over what wasn't ruined, holding the pot in one hand and the skewer in the other. Everyone eventually stopped what they were doing and looked at Sam.

"What do we do now?" said Jim.

"Dinner!" answered Sam, smiling. "And then swimming. I'm feeling pretty confident that I can swim the Sink even if I can't take on those Vipers."

"And pass up a chance for revenge?" Willy barked. "We gotta find Zeke. And then we gotta find *them*."

"Hmm, revenge or swimming, eh?" mused Sam. "Tough choice."

CHOICE

If swimming wins out, turn to page 97.

If thirst for revenge wins out, turn to page 126.

The two cars made their way onto Main Street and moved slowly through the historic old town, then to the highway out of Millersburg. No one spoke. It grew darker and darker as they headed back out to the Sinks. It was nighttime when they finally got there. The old blue car pulled in. Zeke pulled over up the road and turned off the lights. By the moonlight they could see through the trees down into the Sinks.

The old man and Eric poked around where all the bikes had been. Then they climbed back into the car and pulled out onto the road again. "This is very weird," Zeke said as he turned the car around and followed. They drove along without lights for a while until Zeke felt it was safe.

As they drove back, the old blue car turned off and headed for Emeryville. There was nowhere for the car to go, way out in the middle of nowhere, so Zeke let the car get way ahead. "Don't lose them," Jim said with concern.

"Don't worry," Zeke said.

As they rounded a corner into Emeryville, everyone's heart sank. There was no blue car anywhere. "Oh, no!" Willy exclaimed. "They're gone!"

They drove up and down the streets, past the old houses and the parking lots full of kids with nothing else to do. They passed the beat-up, graffiti-covered Emeryville High School and dozens of abandoned cars, but they couldn't find the old blue car. After a long time of searching, Zeke looked down at his watch.

"Oh no! It's after nine! I'm dead meat. Especially for keeping you out."

"We can't go now," Willy and Sam and Jim said at once. "We have to find Eric."

"How?"

None of them had an answer.

Finally, Jim said, "Wait! I have his phone number right here!" He reached into his pocket and pulled out a ragged piece of paper. They pulled over, and the three Ringers climbed out and ran over to a phone. Jim dialed the number as Willy and Sam crowded around.

"Hello," a woman answered.

"Is this Mrs. Donaldson?" Jim said into the receiver.

"Yes, it is. Who is this?"

"This is a friend of Eric's. Is he there?"

"He came home about an hour ago and went straight to bed. I think he's sick. Who is this?"

"This is his friend Jim, from school. Please tell him I'll call tomorrow."

"Good night," Mrs. Donaldson said and hung up abruptly. Jim hung up the phone. They all piled into the car without saying a word. For several miles no one spoke, all of them lost in thought, trying to figure out what had happened.

"Eric's a Viper," Willy said suddenly.

"We don't know that," Jim replied defensively.

"There was something definitely strange happening today," Zeke observed. "But Jim's right. Sounds to me like you guys don't have any idea which end is up. Better listen to Jesus and *judge not*, lest you too be judged."

After they dropped off Sam and Jim, Zeke and Willy headed for home.

Willy looked out at the night and sighed. Jim had said that Eric was going to be back, since Eric was in a special program at school. Willy couldn't wait. Despite what Zeke said, Willy was just *sure* Eric was up to something sneaky.

THE END

Is Willy right? If you aren't sure, turn back to page 1 and make different choices along the way.

Or, turn to page 141.

After a few minutes of quiet, Willy's heart began to slow down. He could hear the breeze moving the trees all around him. He was calming down, so he could tell the difference between a little puff of wind moving a branch and an ax-wielding maniac creeping toward him. "Oh, man," he said, loosening the chin straps of his helmet, "did I just imagine the old guy?"

He stood watching, waiting. After several minutes, he began to ride slowly, nervously, back into the woods.

It was quieter in there; the breeze moved only the branches far overhead. He knew it wouldn't be very far. In his memory it seemed as if the old man was just at the mouth of the woods, but Willy went further and further. Then he came to the bend in the path. This was where he was right before he saw the man, so the man must be behind him. Willy stopped and began to turn his bike around, when a heavy shape fell on him.

"What are you doing following me around down here, you dirt bag?" a harsh voice boomed. Willy fell off his bike and fell back into the bushes. The old man stood over him, holding Willy's bike in one hand as if it were a toy.

The man was huge. He had white hair and wore a baggy black jacket and baggy gray pants. His hands were gnarled and leathery looking. As Willy shimmied backwards into the underbrush, the old man slowly advanced at him.

"I don't take kindly to trespassers, boy!" the old man snarled as he threw Willy's bike aside. "Get outta here!"

"I—I—I," Willy stammered as he got to his feet. Willy was terrified. He had never seen a crazy person before. As he got up to run, the man reached out and grabbed him by the head. Willy's helmet came right off in the man's hand. Willy ran, not bothering to look where he was going. He ran as fast as he could. He looked over his shoulder as he went, and the man just stood there laughing.

And then Willy tripped. The offending box was big and square, and it bruised Willy's left shin in the collision. Willy thought he could see a purse or something like that inside.

"Hey!" the man boomed. Willy looked back, and the man started coming after him.

"Ah!" Willy got up again and ran like the wind.

When Willy came out of the woods this time, he didn't stop to see if the man was following. Willy ran so fast he was winded by the time he reached the front gate. "There's . . . there's," he said, grabbing for his respirator as he pointed back to where he had come from.

Sam clicked off his wristwatch timer and looked at the time. "That's got to be the worst time in the history of Pits motocross," he said, starting to laugh, "and you lost your bike!"

"There's a wild man back there—he took my bike!" Willy said breathlessly. "And he took the helmet!"

"There's a wild man right *here*," Sam corrected, "and he lost *our* helmet."

"No, seriously," Willy said. He reached up and felt

under his chin. It was sore and had a welt. "Look at this." The guys came around and looked at his neck. There was a small gash where the strap had come undone against his neck. "And he had a box with a purse in it."

"Wow," Eric said sarcastically. "Not a *box!*"

"What should we do?" Jim added dramatically. "It's an old man with a box!"

"GUYS!" Willy screeched. Willy's fear had quickly vaporized once he realized that the guy wasn't following him.

"Let's at least go back and check it out. He's not going to murder four of us," suggested Sam.

"No," Jim said, "we should forget about him. There aren't any crazy old men in the woods. It's probably just an old guy going for a walk."

"Whatever we do," said Sam, "we shouldn't just stand here like idiots. Fools or knaves yes, but *not* idiots."

CHOICE ⇛

If they go back and check it out, turn to page 136.

If they forget about it, turn to page 47.

80

F ine," Willy said. "Fine. You girls go off and play in the dump." He shoved Sam in the shoulder and turned to climb on his bike. Sam grabbed his shoulder and tried to turn him back, but Willy pulled himself away.

"Hey, man," said Sam, "we didn't mean to make you mad. Come to the Pits with us."

Willy really *wanted* to join them, but for some reason he was afraid to back down.

Willy didn't look at them. He jerked his bike up and climbed on to it quick and jerky. "I don't need to hang out with a bunch of girls." He pushed himself off and pedaled away from the Freeze.

"Willy!" the Ringers called after him, puzzled, but he didn't look back. He rode across the Common and disappeared down Elm Street.

"That's not like Willy," Jim mused.

"Well, who knows," said Sam. "Maybe he's having a bad day. We'll check on him later."

THE END

Willy's day hasn't been anything like it *could* have been. If you haven't seen some of the other possibilities yet, turn to page 1 and make other choices along the way.

We have to get this out of here," Sam finally said. "We have to take it home or go to the police . . . or *something*."

"What if the old man sees us with the box and comes after us?" Willy cautioned.

"He's not going to see us. If he were still here he would have chased us out by now."

"OK," said Willy. "We'll wrap the box in a shirt and carry it out on my handlebars. Help me lift it up."

They lifted it out of the bushes and carried it toward the mouth of the woods. "Hurry!" Sam said. "Captain Hook is a pirate."

Up ahead they could see the light at the opening of the woods. It was only about twenty yards away when they stopped for a second to put down the box and catch their breath.

They looked at each other, and then into the box, down on all the stolen things—or what they assumed was stolen. There must have been thousands of dollars worth of stuff in the box.

Suddenly, far off behind them they could hear leaves crunching.

Willy and Sam stood bolt upright and turned back toward the way they had come. Way back at the tree where they found the box, they could see a dark figure stooping and digging. Without saying a word, they picked up the box and started to run for the mouth of the trail, which suddenly seemed to be a thousand yards away.

"Hey!" a voice boomed from behind them. They could hear the man running behind them.

Willy and Sam burst out of the woods screaming, "Get the bikes! Get the bikes!" as they crossed the opening. Jim and Eric looked horrified as they stood, dropping their rocks into piles around their feet.

They almost all crashed into one another as they met at the bikes. Sam and Willy wedged the box onto Willy's handlebars. Sam held the bike still as Willy climbed on, then Willy, pedaling slower from the box weight, was passed up by the others as they peeled out. He turned and looked back as he rounded the first big pile of dirt, but the old man was nowhere to be seen. *Lost him!* The three bikes of four kids went barreling down the trail toward the front gate. It looked as if they'd made it.

Then Willy saw him.

The old man had somehow gotten to the top of Boot Hill, the last big hill before the end of the motocross. He stood up there as they rounded the corner and headed straight at Willy, ignoring the others. There was nowhere for Willy to go; the fence blocked one side, and the bottom of Boot Hill blocked the other. Willy's heart raced as he watched the old man coming. *Help me Lord!* he prayed.

All at once the old man hit him, knocking the wind out of Willy and smothering him under a flap of black coat and the old man's bony body. They fell together in the grass by the fence. Willy felt a hard knob press into his shoulder as the man's chest landed on him.

Willy jumped up and the old man looked up. His face was cruel and hard, and his eyes a piercing blue. "So you think you're going to steal this from me, do you?" the old man snapped, reaching for the box. "Get away from here if you don't want to get hurt. That's not a warning. You kids don't know what you're meddling in," he said as he gathered up his stuff.

Seizing the moment, Willy grabbed his bike and pedaled for the gate as hard as he could until he had caught up with the others. *Thank you, Lord,* he prayed, his heart racing.

When he turned back the old man was heading back toward the woods. "Jim, I think we should talk to your grandfather about this," said Willy, turning back to face the guys.

Jim agreed. So did the others.

"Who do you think that old man was?" asked Sam.

"I don't know," Willy said, "but something is going on down there. I wish we could check it out. But something tells me that would be a big mistake."

Indeed it would have been.

THE END

And why? Do you know? If not, turn to page 5 and make other choices along the way.

Or, turn to page 141.

Well," Willy said. The others all turned and looked at him. "If the Vipers are all gone there shouldn't be a problem."

"That's not a very good idea," Eric said.

Willy instantly became annoyed. He didn't like a new guy telling him what to do. "I think that it will be all right," Willy said. "The old guy is, after all, old. And it's not like we're doing an assault on the place. We're just checking it out. He won't even see us."

"But—"

"Come on." Throwing on their clothes, they followed Willy into the brush, heading for the same spot where he and Eric had seen the Vipers and the old man. When they got back to the exact spot, no one was there. All they could see was the clearing, now empty, the big rock up against the steep hillside, and no one around anywhere. "How did the old man leave?" Willy whispered. "We didn't even see him come out."

"This is where you saw them?" Jim said.

"This is exactly where," Eric said.

"I don't see anyone," said Sam. "It looks safe to me." It looked safe to Willy too.

"OK," Willy said, "we need someone to stay behind and keep a lookout." No one wanted to volunteer, so Willy said, "Eric, you stay here. If you see anything, whistle like this." He curled his tongue and whistled like a sparrow.

"I can't do that," Eric said, "I can't curl my tongue."

"Then just whistle like anything you want."

Willy motioned with his arm for the other guys to move out. They came across the clearing crouched over and ready to run if they had to. They moved directly to the big rock and started to poke around a little bit. All around the base of the rock were little tabs of paper and cigarette butts. "Gross," Sam whispered as he poked at them with his toe.

"There's nothing really here," Willy said. "Let's look in the bushes. Maybe they hid something before they left."

They moved over to the bushes at the base of the steep hill. They rummaged around the big one for a second before they felt the whole bush start to move. It was falling to one side. "Stop it! Stop it!" they all whispered to each other frantically as it shifted, but they couldn't stop it. Jumping out of the way, they watched the big, front bush slide to the right, revealing a cave. All three guys looked at each other in disbelief.

"Chris would love this," Willy whispered.

"What should we do?" asked Jim.

"This is not good," said Sam. "This bush-tree thing must weigh a ton. How will we get it back up before someone comes back?"

"If someone comes back, we'll just run. We have to at least check this out." They were all nervous and curious at the same time. Willy looked back at Eric, who waved the all-clear sign and kept looking around. "It looks clear enough," Willy said. "We'll just look inside a little."

They moved around the edge of the fake bush and slid along the hill face until they were crouching down and entering the little cave. It was little, too—only about five feet tall and six feet wide. But it looked deep. In the poor light, they couldn't see any back to it. It could have gone back a hundred yards for all they knew. The walls and ceiling were rough-hewn stone, as if the cave had been dug out or made larger. The dirt on the floor was packed down hard. "I never knew this was here," Sam said. "And I thought I explored every inch of this place."

"It doesn't look like it's been here long—"

"Bishshuhs!" Willy sneezed right out of the blue. Jim and Sam started to laugh. "This dust and dirt is getting to me." Willy pulled out his inhaler and took a puff. "Asthma—it's the pits."

"Let's take a look—"

Just then they heard a car pull up outside the cave entrance. All the guys turned around in total shock. "Where's Eric?" Willy growled. They all started backing deeper into the cave. Through the leaves of the fake bush they could see a man moving around. They backed in deeper. The cave went into the hillside. As they backed in, Willy almost tripped over some boxes, but he caught himself. He breathed a huge, silent sigh of relief, knowing that if he made any noise they'd be discovered. The man hefted the bush-door completely out of his way and peered into the cave. His body filled the entrance and blocked the light. All three guys froze and held their breath. They were about fifteen yards back into the cave and no light fell on them at all. It was completely dark where they were, and they were completely silent. Willy could hear the blood rushing through his ears.

The man grunted and stood again. He backed away from the cave mouth and Willy could see his face. It was a pale, pinkish face, with deep grooves of age running down his cheeks. His hair was pure white and his eyes were sky blue. He looked bigger than he had looked when he was on the rock. Finally he turned, and they heard him getting into his car, but he didn't leave.

"Now's our chance," Jim whispered, almost in a panic. "I'm going to run for it."

"Run where?" Willy said, half-panicked. "We have to wait it out. I don't think he saw us."

"Jim's right," Sam said, getting up. "We have to try to get away now."

CHOICE

If Willy agrees to run, turn to page 48.

If Willy insists on hiding, turn to page 9.

No," Willy suddenly said to Sam. "No, just leave the kid alone. We'll find out about him soon enough."

Sam waited a second to see if Willy really meant it, then turned and stalked away.

Willy frowned, feeling a little anxious about what Sam was going to do. He knew Sam didn't really mean any harm. It was just that when Sam got an idea in his head, it stayed there. He had a one-track mind, and sometimes that track ran over people. He didn't always think of how his actions might affect other people.

That's what Willy was thinking as he walked toward the other guys standing outside the factory. As he came up he could hear them arguing.

"Keeping secrets is for scum!" Sam was saying to Eric.

"What's got into you?" Jim said, stepping in between Eric and Sam. "Why the attitude all of a sudden?"

Eric had a weird look in his eye, fierce and fearless, but without anger. Willy thought that it was kind of the way someone would look at a tough math problem. Suddenly Willy got the sense that it would not be a good idea for Sam to start something with this kid.

"Sam!" said Willy, "mellow out, man. There's no reason to pester the guy."

Sam gave Willy an angry look, then blurted out, "This guy is from *Emeryville*. What do you know about

Emeryville? What do you know about *him?* Emeryville is a dump. They have gang wars every night. What is he doing over here? And what is he hiding?"

Willy drew himself up to defend Eric. "Sam, you are being a complete and total dork. Power down and leave Eric alone!"

Sam opened his mouth to respond, but not before Jim practically yelled, "Sam, you're labeling the guy just the way people label *Hispanics!*"

Sam froze. Sam was Hispanic, and Jim was from Brazil—they *both* knew what it was like to be branded dumb, or not to be trusted, or to be called names for being this or that. And on top of *that,* Willy was black; he knew about prejudice, too. They always said it wasn't fair. It wasn't. And here was Sam, doing it to Eric.

Sam blinked. Looked at Jim. Looked at Eric. Jim's words had doused the fire that had been starting. Everyone began to calm down.

Jim continued, more calmly. "What do you *really* know about Eric—just from the fact that he's from Emeryville? The same thing you know about me, since I'm from Brazil? Or about Willy, since he's black? Eric is a person, and he's our new friend, and that's all that matters."

Eric started to leave.

"Wait!" Willy called and caught up to him. "Wait, Eric." Willy caught Eric by the arm and tried to turn him around. Eric's face was completely expressionless, as if he were watching TV. "Eric, Sam didn't mean any of that. That's just the way he is. He gets an idea and—"

"I don't care how he is," Eric said, deadpan.

"Don't be mad. You'll get used to him—"

"I don't want to get used to him." Eric turned and started to walk away again. Willy caught up with him on the other side of the fence and walked along with him. After a while Eric said, "I don't like it much in Emeryville. I don't think anyone really does. I thought that having the chance to come over here would be great, but all anyone can see is just another dirtbag from Emeryville." Eric stopped and looked Willy in the eye. "Do you know what special program I'm in here in quaint old Millersburg? I'm in an accelerated program, collegiate track. I had to test into it. The schools in Emeryville can barely keep the assaults down, let alone teach you anything." As Eric spoke, he began to talk faster and faster. "And do you know what? I have two sisters who couldn't test out of Emeryville. They're trapped over there, and they can't get out. The only reason I'm here after school today is that I already called home to make sure they were all locked in the house and safe." Willy could see that Eric's eyes were filling with tears. "So I don't need Sam over here in fancy Millersburg telling me that secrets are for scum." He turned and walked off.

Willy let him go.

"I didn't mean it, Willy," Sam said as he came up. "Really—I just got carried away." Willy didn't say anything. He knew Sam probably felt bad, but the damage was done. They hung out in the factory for a while in silence, long after Eric had left.

Finally Willy said to Jim, "Do you think he'll be back?"

"Not today," Jim said sadly. "But I think he'll be around. He has to come over here every day since his mom signed him up to be bused over here."

"That's good," said Willy. "That will give Sam a chance to make it up to him."

Sam started to open his mouth, but Willy stopped him with a look. "Don't you even talk, Emeryville-breath. What did you get all mean for? You were being a dork."

Sam sighed and looked up. He couldn't deny it. All he could do was hope that Eric would give him a chance to apologize.

A bitter pill for wanting to know a secret.

THE END

If you haven't found out Eric's secret, go back to page 5 and keep making new choices along the way.

I think we should follow them," Willy said from the back seat. "We were all out here because this is where I wanted to go and I made Eric be the lookout. I'm responsible."

Zeke turned around in his seat and watched his brother as he spoke. "If you want to do what's good for the people you're responsible for, you should think of their safety. If your friend is in danger, which he probably isn't, he needs someone who can help him. He doesn't need the amateur 'Rescue Rangers' swooping in, getting their heads blown off." Willy looked down at his hands. He knew Zeke was right.

They drove back into Millersburg and stopped at the first pay phone that they could find. Willy stood next to Zeke as he called the police, but the call was pretty short. Zeke told them what happened, gave their address, and said uh-huh about three times, and that was it. He hung up the phone and looked at his brother. "They want us to go home and wait there."

They all went to Zeke and Willy's apartment, where they told Mrs. Washington everything.

Just as the sun was going down, the doorbell rang. It was Eric. A police officer and Mr. Whitehead, Jim's grandfather, stood next to him. The Ringers and Mrs.

Washington welcomed Eric and Mr. Whitehead with a storm of questions as the officer excused himself.

Eric looked a little uneasy but all right. Mr. Whitehead was pleasant but had a serious look on his face, unlike his usual relaxed expression. The small talk ended quickly as soon as he said something to the Ringers that surprised them all: "Jumping to conclusions is your biggest weakness."

It caught them all off guard.

"Huh?"

"What do you mean?"

"You need to get all the facts before you decide what people are like."

They blinked. "But we think Eric is cool," said Jim. The others nodded their agreement.

Mr. Whitehead shook his head. "I wasn't talking about Eric."

They blinked again.

"I mean, it's great that you and Eric have become friends. I'm glad for that. It seems that you have trouble with the people you don't quite get close to. The ones you observe . . . from a distance."

Willy, Sam, and Jim furrowed their brows in thought as they tried to figure this out. Who had they seen that day from a distance? Bill Grossman, the Vipers, and . . .

"You mean the old man?" Willy asked suddenly, not really expecting to be right.

Mr. Whitehead nodded.

"You *know* him?" asked Jim.

Mr. Whitehead shook his head.

"You mean you *don't* know him?" asked Willy.

Mr. Whitehead shook his head.

"So you *don't* know him, you just know we shouldn't assume that he feeds Vipers?" suggested Sam.

Mr. Whitehead smiled. "Young Samuel, you are growing in wisdom."

Sam grinned widely. "I know, Kimosabe."

"But you are not yet humble enough," Mr. Whitehead added. Willy and Jim laughed. Sam blushed.

"He's saying the old man isn't who you think he is." Eric finally spoke up. Everyone looked at him.

"Then who *is* he?" the Ringers all said at once.

Eric smiled. "Can't tell you."

"What?"

"Like I said," Mr. Whitehead said again, standing up, "you guys jump to conclusions too fast. You need to get all the facts first." He smiled at them.

"Herewith let it be known that we seeketh to get all the facts, Kimosabe!" Sam said with energy, looking right at Mr. Whitehead.

"I don't *have* all the facts, *Kimosabe*," the old pastor replied. "I only know that your conclusions about him come from what you saw with your *eyes*, and not with your *understanding*."

Sam sighed heavily and collapsed on the couch. "I think my understanding needs glasses."

"So the old man isn't messed up with the Vipers?" Willy asked, in almost total disbelief.

"That's right," said Mr. Whitehead.

"Not possible," Willy said automatically.

"Very possible," Mr. Whitehead said as he reached for the doorknob. "Gentlemen, I must go. Jean is waiting for me."

The guys said good-bye, and he left.

Before the door even closed, the Ringers were pelting Eric with questions. "Who *is* the old man?" "What did he do to you?" "Did he torture you?" "Where have you been?"

Eric couldn't help but smile at his newfound celebrity status. He wasn't usually the center of so much attention. But he insisted on keeping the secret. "Nope, can't say. Can't say," he said, shaking his head.

"Can't you even give us a *clue?*" Sam pleaded. "A teeny-tiny sentence fragment?"

Finally, Eric held up his hands. "OK, OK," he finally said. Everyone else hushed and leaned closer. "I'll tell you." All fell silent.

Eric cleared his throat. "You know that bus in the Dead Sink?" Eric said, then started to laugh.

They all nodded.

"That old man was the bus driver."

In the short second it took them to get the joke, Eric tried to get past them to the door, knowing that once they got it, he didn't have a chance. But he never made it. Sam leaped on him while screaming something about torturing it out of him, Willy piled on Sam, and Jim leaped on top of Willy. A clump of fourteen-year-olds fell on the floor in a heap as Willy, Sam, and Jim squished Eric. It was several minutes of uncontrollable squishing and laughing before they were all able to breathe again. Finally, the guys peeled themselves off each other in exhaustion.

Eric pointed at Sam. "Gotcha!"

"Boomeranged!" Sam said, accepting the bad taste of his own medicine.

The guys eventually decided to let Eric have his secret. It was Friday evening. The weekend was ahead of them. They had a new friend and two days to show him around.

That gave them plenty of time to torture it out of him.

THE END

Have you figured out who the old man is? If not, turn back to page 5 and make other choices along the way.

Or, turn to page 141.

They decided to put dinner on hold and cool off in the Sinks. They rode down the slope and parked their bikes under a thick bush at the corner of the Dead Sink. As they began stripping down to their swim trunks under their pants, Eric asked, "Why do you call the right one the Dead Sink?"

"Well," said Sam, "that's a good question." Sam took Eric by the elbow and led him slowly along the bank of the Dead Sink. Eric shoved his hands deep into his swimsuit pockets. "A long time ago, when these Sinks were just freshly dug, a group of grade-school kids came out here to go swimming on a hot September day. They piled into the bus and drove all the way out here on a field trip. But they were in for a terrible surprise." He lowered his voice as he spoke, slowing their walking.

Willy and Jim were in their swim trunks and followed to listen to Sam's story.

"The school bus was being driven by a crazy old man, an escapee from a nearby insane asylum. Instead of slowing down when they got here to the Sinks, he started to speed up. The kids in the bus screamed as the bus rocked and rolled over the hills, crashing through the trees and underbrush, the crazy old man laughing maniacally. And then, they broke through the clearing, hit the rise back there, and flew through the air." They stopped, Willy not noticing until just now that they had rounded the corner of the Dead Sink and were standing on its far side. Sam stood silently, staring into the dark water.

"Well," Eric said, "what happened?"

"The bus hit the water and sank to the bottom." He pointed into the water. They all looked. Under the water, just a few feet off from the shore, they could see the rear end of a bus, the yellow fading to a light brown, its big square windows looking up from under the water. A little bit of green slime coated the whole thing.

"They say," Sam continued, "that if you look closely," he leaned closer to the water, holding Eric's elbow, "you can see the faces of the kids' ghosts down in the water, looking up through the windows." Just then Sam shoved Eric toward the water, but not hard enough for him to fall in. Eric's face turned a little white as he slid down the bank toward the submerged bus. Both his arms flailed wildly as he tried to keep his balance. The other guys laughed and rushed down the bank to join Sam and Eric and to help him back up. Eric still hadn't caught his balance. When Sam came up behind him, Eric reached back for him. Sam screamed. Willy could see that Eric had caught Sam by the neck as he was trying to climb back up, and that Sam was trying to push him away. Then he saw it.

Eric's right hand was different from his other hand. It was undersized, with only three pale gray fingers. Eric was waving it in Sam's face, trying to climb up the bank.

Willy stopped laughing.

"Get away from me!" Sam said, shoving Eric back down the bank away from him. The three guys stood over

Eric, who sat still on the bank. After an awkward moment, Jim pushed past the others and climbed down to help Eric up, but Eric didn't want to come. He just sat there and stared at the ground. Finally, Jim got Eric up and they climbed the bank.

"Way to go," said Jim as they passed.

"What?" Sam said defensively.

Willy grabbed Sam's arm. "Apologize, you tulip head!"

CHOICE

If Sam apologizes, turn to page 30.

If Sam refuses, turn to page 133.

Come over here," Willy said. "I want to talk to you."

"What, what?"

Willy could tell by the tone of Sam's voice that he was getting impatient with all of this spy and secret stuff. Willy thought it was getting a little old, too.

Jim looked over his shoulder as he and Eric went into the factory. Willy could tell that he was thinking, *Don't tell the secret!*

"What is it with this Eric guy, anyway?" Sam pressed. "I don't get all this quiet stuff. We don't normally keep secrets."

"It's not like you think," Willy said, much quieter than Sam. "I have a feeling Eric is an all-right guy." He looked at his own feet as he spoke. "If Chris were here he would give the guy a chance, probably. . . ."

"You're not telling me something," said Sam. "That's why you and Jim were outside. He told you something about Eric . . . or you saw something before that you don't want me in on. What's going on?"

"Sam, just because we're friends doesn't mean we can blab everybody's secrets to each other. Eric doesn't *belong* to us, you know." Willy was starting to get annoyed at Sam's persistence.

Sam said nothing. Willy waited for some kind of

response. He didn't want to be unfair to Eric, but he also valued Sam's friendship.

Finally, Willy said, "Look, if you have to know I'll tell you. But you *have* to promise total, complete, impossible-to-torture-out-of-you secrecy! OK?"

"OK," said Sam.

"OK," said Willy, and he leaned close and whispered, "Eric's got a deformed hand."

Sam's eyes bugged out. "No way!"

"Yes way. He only has three fingers."

"Hey you guys!" Jim called out the window. Willy and Sam looked guiltily up at him.

The look on Jim's face grew angry. "You told him," he whispered hoarsely at Willy.

"It's OK," Willy pleaded. "Sam's a Ringer."

"Willy, I can't believe you! That doesn't make it OK." Jim pulled his head back in. Willy and Sam could hear the two guys upstairs crashing around.

Willy felt terrible. Suddenly he realized that he had been a pretty lousy friend to Eric. "Sam, *please* don't tell anybody else. *Please?*"

"All right, dude. I won't mess up the way you did."

Willy looked down.

Sam noticed. "Hey, just kidding. It's all right—Eric's secret is safe with me."

Without another word the two started to head up the stairs. Just then they heard terrible crashes and shouts coming from the floors above. It sounded as if there were more than just two voices coming from the floors above. Willy and Sam broke into a run up the stairs.

102

At the top of the stairs Willy saw something that made his skin crawl. Three of the Vipers were pushing around Jim and Eric. They wore the Viper colors and black jeans. They looked a year or two older than the Ringers. They surrounded Jim and Eric and were shoving them around. Willy started to run at the ruckus, but Sam grabbed his arm and motioned him to walk calmly over. They approached coolly. Willy said, "What do you think you're doing up here?"

The one guy stepped around Jim and came over to Willy. He was about six inches taller, but the same build. "Who do you think you are, king squirrel?"

Fear started to overcome Willy. All he really wanted to do was get out and get the other guys out. He vividly remembered Jake mentioning the Vipers at Camp Silverlake, and they didn't sound like the happy-go-lucky kind.

But in this situation Willy couldn't see any easy way out. He couldn't just wave bye and walk away; the Vipers wouldn't let them. And Willy knew—at least in his head—that he shouldn't fight. After all, Jesus said to "turn the other cheek." For the most part, it always worked.

He wasn't so sure this time.

The three Vipers squared off with the four guys and stared menacingly at them.

CHOICE ➡

If Willy decides to try to fight their way out of this, turn to page 52.

If he decides to try to talk their way out of this, turn to page 22.

Willy wheeled about on his bike and started pedaling back to the guys. Whatever had just happened, Willy had a strange nervous feeling in his stomach. What had happened to the man? Who was he?

Willy didn't bother jumping any more hills. He just rode straight around the last bend and pedaled right up to the guys. As he rode up, they all looked a bit puzzled and Sam started to laugh.

"You got to be kidding me," Sam said. "Your *grandmother* could have done better than that. You didn't even come over Boot Hill, the granddaddy of them all. My time kills yours by a year."

Willy was shaking his head, climbing off his bike as he came to a stop. "Forget about the time," he said impatiently. "I saw something freaky out there."

"What?"

Willy whipped off his helmet and dropped it by his bike as he spoke. "When I was going over the Killer Trail, I went through the woods right before Boot Hill. You're not going to believe what I saw in there. It was amazing."

"Crockamonkies?" joked Sam.

"I almost ran over this old guy, nearly broke him in half!" Willy said ignoring him.

"Old crockamonkies!"

All the guys burst into laughter. "You almost killed a

pedestrian, and that's what you were so psyched about?"
Sam laughed as he slapped Willy on the back. Eric looked
closely at Jim, then began to laugh as soon as Jim burst out
laughing.

"Did he threaten you with his cane?" Jim asked.

"Did he run after you with an ax?" Sam followed.

"No, his dentures!"

"He was probably burying his loot from a bank job,"
Eric said, laughing.

"Very funny." Willy was annoyed. "I almost break a guy
in half in the woods, and you guys get big yucks out of it.
I'm telling you the guy came out of nowhere and then just
disappeared. And what's an old guy doing rooting around
here in the Pits? This isn't exactly the Common, you know."
He picked up the helmet and tossed it to Jim. "Put this in
the knapsack and throw it in the bushes by the gate. We
gotta go see what the old man was doing."

They all rode around the edge of the motocross and
came to the entrance of the woods. "What did he look
like?" they asked Willy as they went.

"I didn't get a good look at him because it was so fast,
but he had really white hair." Willy stopped and looked at
the others.

Sam rolled his eyes.

Nothing had changed since Willy came busting out a
few minutes earlier. It was very quiet. No old man. No
white hair.

"I'm going in," said Willy.

"Me too," said Sam.

Willy looked over at Jim and Eric; they weren't

moving. "You guys stay here and keep a lookout. Get some rocks in case we need them." It was a good thing to say; he figured that Chris would have told them to do the same thing. Jim and Eric immediately stooped to gather rocks as Willy and Sam crept into the woods.

It was so quiet that Willy thought every step thundered crunches of dried leaves through the dim woods. They made their way up the path, staying close to each other. "This is where I saw the old man. I almost crashed right into him."

Willy was crouching down, but Sam stood tall and straight, his hands on his hips, shaking his head. "This is the kind of thing *I* would pull," he said. "You don't expect me to believe this story, do you?"

Willy didn't answer but headed into the bushes and started looking around. This time Sam didn't follow. After a few seconds, Willy returned and said, "Well, maybe this will help you to believe." He held up a pearl necklace that seemed to be three feet long.

"Whoa," Sam said as he lunged into the bushes toward Willy. There, at the base of a tree, half covered with dead leaves, was a wooden box. Willy and Sam started to rummage through it. "I can't believe it. There's all kinds of stuff in here: tape players, jewelry, credit cards, wallets, money!" Willy held up a wad of cash. Their eyes bulged as they saw it.

"What are we gonna do, Willy?"

Willy answered by interpreting Sam's question for him. "You mean, does it belong to that old man? Or do we just leave it here in the middle of the Pits?"

Sam nodded and thought for a moment. "We'd better leave it."

"OK," Willy agreed. He put the wad of money back in the box. "Just leave it here, in the middle of the woods," he thought out loud. "In the middle of the woods? Wait a minute, are you crazy? This is a little miniature Fort Knox right here! Suppose an aardvark comes and eats this stuff. We can't just *leave* it here!"

"But it doesn't belong to us," said Sam.

"Well, who *does* it belong to?" Willy asked impatiently.

"I don't know. *You're* the one who nearly ran over an insane old man—"

"I didn't say he was insane."

"Whatever! Willy, you want us to just pick up this box and haul it home? 'Hi Mom! Guess what I found today in the woods!'"

"OK, OK, so we'll leave it here."

Neither said anything. Neither moved, either.

"Shall we go now?" Willy prodded, forcing Sam to make the first move.

Sam stared at the box. "Willy?"

"Yes?"

"How many wallets do you have?"

"I don't have any wallets."

"How many does your dad have?"

Willy shrugged. "One."

Sam nodded. "Mine too. This box has *several*. Like it was a community wallet pantry or something."

A light bulb went on in Willy's head. He whistled a "you're right" type of whistle.

"Me thinkum this box not tiny Fort Knox, Kimosabe," Sam said in his Tonto voice, "but budget treasure chest of Captain Hook."

Willy looked around nervously. What Sam said made sense. If he was right, who knows when Captain Hook might come back to bury his treasure. "So what do we do?" he finally asked.

CHOICE➡

If they decide to take the box, turn to page 81.

If they leave the box, turn to page 119.

Normally Willy would have just gone along with Zeke because he trusted his judgment, but this time something just screamed inside him not to do what Zeke wanted to do. He decided that he wanted to look around *first*.

"No!" Willy said loudly from the back of the car, "we don't have time. And I think we ought to start at the factory."

Zeke didn't say anything for a second, and then, "OK, this is the plan: We'll call the police as soon as we hit town, then the four of us will cruise around that part of town until we find something."

They called as soon as they rolled into Millersburg, then headed straight for the factory and the Pits. They turned onto the street and slowed down. Willy's intuition was right; no sooner had they turned the corner than they all spotted an old blue car with a Virginia license plate starting with *SC*. It was parked across from the factory, in front of one of the old beat-up houses lining the street. They pulled up along the curb way up the street and sat quietly, waiting to see what would happen next.

"Zeke," Jim said finally in the silent car, "what if something's happening to Eric right now, while we're sitting here?"

Zeke didn't say anything. He just looked at his watch and shook his head. "Don't know. We've done what we can.

We could pray." It was starting to get dark; the shadows
across the street were long and gray. "Once it gets dark, we
can forget about staying down here too long," Zeke
mumbled.

Just as he said it, the old man came out of the house
with Eric. They all expected to see Eric tied up or in
handcuffs, but he was walking casually alongside the old
man. All four in the car slunk down and watched as they
came out.

"What do we do now?" Sam whispered.

"*Watch* and pray," said Jim.

"Hmm," Zeke agreed.

Everyone looked at Zeke, but he didn't say a word.
Eric and the old man walked across the street and they
both got into the car. Eric wasn't trying to run for it; he just
walked around the other side and got in.

"Something is weird here," Zeke said.

"Willy," said Sam matter-of-factly. Willy poked him.

"Let's wait for the police," said Zeke. "They should be
here any minute."

"No, no, no," Willy protested, "we have to follow
them!"

"Doesn't this look weird to any of you?" said Zeke.
"Why doesn't this Eric try to get away? He's free and clear
on the other side of the car. He's had three chances to get
away since he came out of the house. How well do you
know this guy? This looks very weird to me—which
doesn't surprise me, with *you* guys involved." Zeke shook
his head.

Willy and Sam looked at each other. Was Eric mixed

110

up with the Vipers? What if Eric was in this from the start? Willy felt a chill. But what if Eric *wasn't* involved? Then what should they do?

The blue car didn't move the whole time they sat there thinking about their next move, as if the old man were waiting.

Suddenly the taillights came on and the car pulled away from the curb.

"Follow them!" Willy and Sam said at the same time.

"OK, but I don't think this is the best idea in the world," Zeke said as he turned on the engine.

Turn to page 74.

Ugh, gross," Sam started to laugh nervously. He stepped away from the others and made a funny face. "It's the claw! It's the claw!"

Jim looked up, his eyes wide in shock and embarrassment.

Willy was surprised, too, but he couldn't stop himself from giggling.

Eric had no expression. His face was still red from having the wind knocked out of him. He pushed Jim away, and, staggering, he looked hard at Sam, who was still laughing.

The look on Eric's face stopped Sam cold in his smirks. Eric turned and started to walk off slowly. They could all hear his heavy breathing as he started walking up the street.

Willy turned on Sam. "Well, that was really smooth!"

"I didn't notice that you were too straight-faced," answered Sam. He looked down at his feet and shook his head. "Oh, man, do I feel stupid. I didn't mean to say it; it just slipped out."

Jim looked angrily from Sam to Willy. "I don't know what gets into you sometimes. What are you looking for a speck in his eye for? Do you think it's easy being Eric?" Jim picked up his bike and straddled it as he pushed off. He rode quickly through the gate and turned in the direction that Eric had gone.

After a few quiet minutes, Willy sighed and walked slowly over to his bike. Even though he hadn't said anything to Eric, he felt stupid. Sam followed, and they both picked up their bikes at the same time. "Well," said Sam, "that was lame."

"Yeah," Willy agreed. They climbed on their bikes and rode slowly through the gate.

"Let's catch up with them," Sam suggested. "Maybe we can make it up to Eric somehow."

"OK," answered Willy excitedly. They took off to find Eric and Jim.

Wherever their Brazilian friend and his new buddy had disappeared to, they had disappeared good. Sam and Willy's quest consumed about an hour, until hunger pains started to drive them crazy. They decided to quit and went home for dinner.

Meanwhile, Eric went home, too—a lot earlier than he had planned. His brief get-acquainted time with Sam and Willy convinced him that Jim's friends were no different from all the others who had rejected him, whether or not they lived in "quaint, historic" Millersburg, and whether or not they were "Ringers" for Jesus. Jim's apologies for Sam and Willy only partly blunted the hurt.

Eric had heard it all before, and he didn't care.

THE END

The consequences of Sam and Willy's actions are severe. What if they had decided to be friends with Eric? Turn to page 27 and see what a difference it would have made.

"Listen, guys," Willy pleaded, "it was just a dumb joke that got out of hand. No, no, not out of hand, I didn't mean that. Eric, don't be mad, that was just Sam being Sam. I've known him for years; he's just a blockhead sometimes."

Eric didn't look up, and Jim just kept getting dressed.

"Listen," Willy tried again. "This is stupid. It was just a stupid mistake that could have happened to anybody."

"Eric doesn't think it was so stupid," Jim pointed out.

Willy turned to Sam for help. "Sam, you didn't mean what you said. Apologize."

Sam got to his feet, and grabbing his clothes, he climbed on his bike. Without a word he rode past the others and stopped at the top of the rise. All the guys looked up at him. Sam looked like he wanted to say something, but then he just turned and rode away.

Jim shook his head as he finished dressing. He climbed on his bike. Then he and Eric rode up the hill and out of sight.

Willy walked over to the edge of Dead Sink and sat down. He skipped small rocks across the surface. *Oh well,* he thought, *so much for an adventure this weekend. Maybe nothing at all was supposed to get off the ground. Maybe there was nothing happening at all.* After a while he got up and rode his bike out of the Sinks too. About half way home he ran into Sam.

Sam climbed out of the trees on the side of the road and waited as Willy approached. Sam was silent for several minutes. Finally he said, "El Jerko strikes again."

"Amen to that, brother."

"What do you think I should do?"

"Apologize!" Sam said it at the same time Willy did. They laughed.

THE END

For more adventures with Willy and Sam, turn to page 1 and make different choices along the way.

Or, turn to page 141.

Well," said Eric, "maybe you could let me borrow it and I could ride around and see what this place is like, first."

"Maybe," said Sam, "or maybe you could just get it over with and jump Boot Hill."

"Maybe you should let him do it in his own way," Jim said as he pushed between the two with his bike. "Come on, Eric, let's go look around. We can motocross all day. Let's check out the factory while it's still light." Eric slid behind Jim and the two rode off. Willy and Sam looked at each other, puzzled.

"What's with Jim?" Sam blurted out.

Willy climbed on his bike and shook his head. "That kid Eric has got something weird going on in his life," he said. "Maybe you should cut him some slack and have some fun."

"I was just kidding around. What do you think he's hiding in his coat pocket?"

Willy pulled his bike to a stop and looked at Sam. "I wish you'd just drop it, Sam. The more we talk about it, the more he starts giving me the creeps."

"Listen," said Sam, "when I was little, I knew a kid from Emeryville. He was like Eric, all weird and secretive, but he was different. He was always hiding something in his lunch box at school, always looking inside and never coming near anybody. One day there was this terrible smell in class and the teacher tracked it to the lunch boxes. Do you know what was in that kid's box?"

"No, what?" asked Willy, hanging on every word.

"A dead hamster. That kid was carrying around a dead hamster with all his food. He said his older brother killed a whole litter and the one he was carrying around was the one he was supposed to have." Sam burst into laughter.

"That is *so* gross!" Willy started to laugh too. "That's not a real story," he said as they started to walk toward the factory.

"Maybe it is and maybe it isn't," Sam replied. "But I'll tell you this: that kid from Emeryville never came back to our class. He was the last kid I saw bused in from that town."

"Do you think that Eric's got a dead animal in his jacket?"

"He *is* from Emeryville."

"Come on," Willy laughed, "let's go find Jim and the Hamster Man."

Sam and Willy could see Jim and Eric by the factory, leaning Jim's bike against the wall by the door and waiting for them to catch up. Suddenly Sam caught Willy by the arm and stopped him just as they got to the fence.

"What?" asked Willy.

Sam looked him in the eye. "I just thought of something else. We really should find out more about this kid. If he *is* from Emeryville, he could be an alien."

Willy smiled and pulled away. "You're being a fool, Sam. Just let the kid be."

"Wait. This is *our* club. Suppose we decide to ask him in. Then we would have to know all about him anyway."

Willy didn't like the sound of this; it was like they were going to interrogate Eric. He frowned and shook his head.

"Well," Sam said hurriedly, "let's at least hit Jim for some information."

They were standing by the fence that ran across the back of the building. Sam just stood staring at Willy, making him feel uncomfortable. Willy looked a long time at Jim and Eric by the entrance. He wasn't really sure what to do, but he knew that Sam was getting impatient.

CHOICE ⇒

If Willy promises to ask Jim about Eric, turn to page 134.

If Willy lets it drop, turn to page 88.

Let's just leave it where it is and tell the police," said Sam.

"OK, I can live with that. Come on, let's cover it back up."

The two friends hurriedly covered the box with leaves and twigs. When that was done they headed straight for the light without looking back.

"Let's get outta here!" Willy shouted as soon as they cleared the woods, and the four jumped on their three bikes and started out of the Pits. Willy and Sam explained as they rounded Boot Hill and headed out through the gate.

They just started down toward the Common and the police station when a cruiser turned the corner and headed right for them. As soon as the officer saw the guys he turned on his lights and pulled up to the curb in front of them. He stepped out and pulled on his cap as he motioned for the Ringers to pull up to the curb.

"Officer Gary!" the guys shouted to him. They knew him because he coached their baseball team. He also "arrested" them from time to time.

"What are you boys doing this afternoon?"

"There's a man in the Pits! He's a burglar! He has all kinds of wallets!" All the guys shouted at the officer at once.

"Hold it, hold it," Officer Gary said. "What man is *where?*" He nodded his head and listened carefully as Willy described the whole thing. "I almost ran over a man back in the Pits—that's the factory yard—anyway, we went back and looked to find the man but he was gone, but we found a box of stuff, full of radios and jewelry and money, and credit cards and wallets, and we thought about taking it, but we weren't sure, so we came to get you."

Officer Gary blinked. "Are you sure?"

Willy nodded his whole upper body.

"It is the *truth,* Kimosabe Gary, the most obnoxious truth," Sam added.

Officer Gary grew quiet. "What did you say the man looked like?" he asked.

As Willy described the old man, the policeman's expression grew more and more grim.

"What is it, Officer Gary? Does the old man fit the description of a thief you've been tracking?" Willy asked.

Pausing for a moment, Officer Gary decided how much he could tell the boys. "Listen, boys, you've stumbled on something, all right. But the bad guys aren't necessarily the ones you think they are." Pulling them closer in a circle, he continued. "I'm telling you this because I want you to keep what you've seen to yourselves. That old man is an undercover cop. He's been working on breaking up a gang that's starting to move into Millersburg. What you found is the loot gang members are trading him for drugs. This is heavy-duty stuff, not ballroom dances. So you had better stay away from that area and away from that box till this clears up. What's in that box is evidence, and we need it to break this thing.

"I'm telling you this because I trust you, and I don't want you getting mixed up in this. So play it cool for a while, and keep what you've seen and what I've told you under wraps. This is one thing you guys shouldn't go 'Ring'ing the town with."

The idea of gangs roving around their beloved Pits was a downer to all the guys. They had had lots of fun times riding around there, and now all that was put on hold—and right before the summer, too. They had all heard about gangs, and knew about some at school, but for the most part gangs had stayed out of Millersburg.

At least until now.

THE END

What would have happened to the guys if they hadn't run into Officer Gary? Would they have met up with any gangs? Turn back to page 25 and make different choices along the way to find out!

Or, turn to page 141.

Willy stood still for a moment, thinking about the consequences of what they could do. He remembered what his grandmother Hattie always told him: Just because you *can* do something doesn't mean you *should* do something.

"Well?" Sam said.

"Look guys, this guy and the Vipers seem like they could do some damage," Eric offered. "I don't think we should head over there."

"Ah, man—," Sam started, but Eric cut him off.

"Look, that guy over there could be a real criminal. We saw him passing out guns."

"Guns?" Jim and Sam both yelled at once.

Willy turned and looked hard at Eric. He didn't remember seeing any guns, just brown packages. Maybe he had seen them wrong, or just didn't know what they were. "Are you sure you saw guns over there? I only remember—"

"Believe me. I come from Emeryville. Those guys were doing some pretty heavy stuff."

"Then let's get out of here," Willy finally said.

The guys all threw on their clothes and got on their bikes. They pedaled out of the Sinks and headed for town. At every turn Willy expected to see a truck full of Vipers come down on them, but they saw no one. About a mile outside of town they ran across Zeke. He was out on a cruise in the

"Batmobile," his totally black Chrysler. Zeke and Shorty pulled over, and all the guys gathered around the car.

"What's happening short stuff?" Zeke said to Sam as they all stopped. Willy came up to the window of the car and looked down at his brother seriously.

"Hey, Zeke," Willy said, "we were just up at the Sinks and saw something."

"What was that? Not girls I hope." Zeke reached over and slapped Willy in the arm, and they both laughed.

"Of course not, silly," said Sam. *"Women."*

"No, we saw some Vipers, and they were buying stuff from some old guy."

Zeke's smile disappeared from his face. He looked up at his brother seriously. "This isn't funny. Get home and tell Mom and Dad. I'll be back later." The Batmobile moved away slowly, then accelerated quickly as Zeke pulled away.

All four of the guys went over to Willy's apartment. They waited uneasily.

"What if something happens to Zeke?" Jim said, sounding worried.

"Nothing will happen," Willy said nonchalantly. He sat for as long as he could, wondering about Eric, but Willy finally had to ask how Eric knew so much. Willy didn't want to ask him in front of the other guys, so he called Eric out to the kitchen. When they were alone, Willy asked, "Why did you say those guys had guns? We didn't see anything like that."

Eric sighed and leaned against the refrigerator. "You don't need to see some stuff to know it's there. Sometimes it's safer to assume the worst and stay away. I live in

Emeryville. The street I live on is pretty bad. A lot of bums live there. And there's a house on my street that always has something bad going on with the police. Living with my mom I've seen a lot."

"Is that why you come here to go to school?"

"It's part of a busing program. But my sisters are still stuck over there. My mom is trying to get them out, too. She may be single, but she's smart. She wants us out of there, but we're stuck a lot of the time."

Willy put his hand on Eric's shoulder. "You're not stuck all the time, dude. You're welcome over here whenever." They started back into the living room where the other guys were. "Maybe Mr. Whitehead can help your mom find a place to stay here in Millersburg. It's a lot safer." Eric smiled as Zeke finally came in. "What did you find?" Willy asked excitedly.

Zeke came over and sat down on the couch. "What did I find?" said Zeke, "what did I find? Zip. The place was as boring as a date with Sam."

"No one's about to date me, bonehead," Sam said, countering Zeke's joke as he flung a magazine in Zeke's direction.

"If you guys did see something," Zeke said as he got up, "I want you to stay away from there for a while." He pointed his finger at Willy and said, "All right?"

"Yeah," they all said. After Zeke left, the guys decided to hit the Freeze. Yeah, they would stay away, for a while. But they all knew that something was up, and that sooner or later they would find out what.

THE END

Do *you* know who the old man is who Willy and Eric saw? And is Eric telling the truth? If you're still not sure, turn back to page 40 and make different choices along the way.

Or, turn to page 141.

Do you think revenge is really a good idea?" Jim asked. "All that's gonna do is get us all in trouble. Vengeance isn't our business anyway."

"I don't care," said Willy. "First thing we gotta do is find *Zeke,* and then we gotta go after *them.*"

Jim and Sam looked at each other with concern as Willy stormed down the hill, leaving everyone behind. He climbed onto his bike and, without waiting, pedaled down the hill and straight across the divide. He was out of the Sinks before Eric had a chance to turn his awkward old bike around, last to start chasing after him.

Willy was a good distance ahead of them when he rushed into the Freeze and sat down to catch his breath. Betty, who ran the shop and was a friend of the Ringers, turned around and looked at Willy with amazement.

"Have you seen Zeke?" Willy finally blurted out.

Betty shook her head.

"I need to see my brother. It's important." But Betty hadn't seen Zeke all day.

The other guys finally caught up with Willy, who then led them on a search for his brother. The guys followed him around for the better part of an hour. They went everywhere: to the church, to the Pits, to Larry's Laundromat, even to the city hall and the police station. Somewhere along the way they lost Eric; Jim dropped out to keep him company. Willy was getting ready to ride out to George Mason University when Sam, Willy's only surviving follower, finally dug in his heels.

"Willy, has it ever occurred to you that this is a waste of time? We already lost Jim and Eric!"

It was only then that Willy noticed that Eric was gone. "Where is he?" Willy said.

"He had to go," Sam answered. "Probably to have dinner, like we should've done. Now it's almost dark."

Willy looked up at the sky. The sun was almost below the horizon; the day was ending.

Willy swiped his face and sighed. This was a waste of time, all right. A waste of time and a hopeless cause. Willy hated giving up.

He looked at Sam. "I just wish we could get back at those hoseheads for trashing our fort."

"I know what you mean, Kimosabe." Sam paused, then got a thought. "Maybe we should pray for them!"

"Hey, yeah!"

Willy and Sam laughed hard. What a crazy idea—praying for your enemies!

The two Ringers turned their bikes and headed for Millersburg at a leisurely pace. They were tired. Biking around looking for revenge takes a lot out of you.

128

THE END

Does Willy ever find the Vipers, or do the Vipers find *him?* Go back to page 1 and make different choices along the way to continue with the adventure.

Or, turn to page 141.

Scramble!" Willy yelled as all three guys came tearing out of the cave. As soon as they came out, Jim and Sam ran right into each other, and Willy had to help them up. By the time he got them on their feet the two men were over their shock and came running right at them. The last thing Willy saw before the cop landed on him was Sam's back disappearing into the woods.

The cop picked Willy up off the ground and led him back to the car. The officer looked hard at him. "You're in an awfully dangerous situation, son. Do you know what's going on out here?"

Willy shook his head.

"Did you overhear what we were talking about?"

Willy shook his head.

The old man stood behind the cop and shook his head also, but it was a slow, mean shake of the head that scared Willy.

"Well, son," the cop said again, obviously annoyed. But he was interrupted by a small miracle. Through the trees Willy heard the familiar hum of the Batmobile. Willy's heart jumped.

Zeke's car came to a stop a few yards from the cop and Zeke jumped out. Willy could tell he was worried. "What's going on here?" he asked in a serious tone. "Is my brother in trouble?"

The officer walked calmly over to Zeke. "Your brother has trespassed on a posted off-limits area. Are you a legal custodian of this boy?"

Zeke laughed. "Not exactly. I'm his older brother. Mom sent me out here to tell the guys that a storm might be rolling in tonight."

While Zeke talked to the cop, the old man came over and looked at Willy, who involuntarily stared back, scared and unsure what would happen next. "You don't know what you've stumbled across here, son. You and your little friends could have been responsible for a lot of trouble for a lot of people. You can just thank your lucky stars that the Vipers didn't show up." The old man led Willy over to Zeke and the cop. "You and your friends would do well to get out of here and not come back for a long time." The old man turned and headed back to his car.

The cop jerked his head back toward the old man and continued with what he was saying to Zeke. "That's Special Officer Angstrom. He's not the friendliest guy in the world." Turning to Willie, he said, "Like I was saying to your brother, this is a bad place for you to be. You could be seriously injured, or killed. I want you out of here, and I want you to promise not to return."

Without hesitating, Willy nodded his head, too scared to speak.

The officer turned and started walking away, then turned again and added, this time with a look of concern on his face on top of his rough tone, "And if you happen to see any Vipers, or any of the Emeryville gangs on your way home, stay away. All they do is ruin nice kids like you."

Willy grabbed his bike and got a ride home alone with Zeke. Later, he found out that the other guys had hidden and then rode home through the back roads and woods. He missed not having been with them, but was thankful that his brother happened to show up. He didn't want to think about what could have happened.

"Those guys are the big leagues, Will," Zeke said. "Whatever you saw back there, you'd better not tell to *anybody.*"

"Yeah," Willy answered.

"I mean it, Will. Those dudes are about to ice a gang or something, and they don't need us messing it up."

Willy nodded. It was a good thing he respected Zeke enough to do exactly as his brother suggested. Bad for the Vipers, but a good thing for Willy.

Of course, Willy didn't really know what he had seen—just a box in a cave, a cop, and an old guy talking about fences and Vipers. But that was enough.

When they got back to Millersburg, Zeke insisted on staying with Willy until the others got back. That was OK with him. He felt kind of cool hanging out with his brother. Zeke even bought him some chocolate macadamia ice cream.

About an hour later Jim, Sam, and Eric showed up. They looked tired. Then Willy and Zeke told them what had happened, and Zeke persuaded them to swear to secrecy for their own good. Then Zeke took off.

"Why don't you guys all sleep over," Willy said as they came out of the Freeze. "The weekend is just starting, and tomorrow we can go to the Pits!"

132

"What are the Pits?" Eric asked.

"That's where we motocross," answered Jim. "But don't worry—it won't be nearly as wild as the Sinks."

THE END

Have you been to the Pits yet? If not, turn to page 1 and make different choices along the way.

Or, turn to page 141.

What do you mean, apologize?" said Sam. When Sam's jokes backfired this badly, it was hard for him to take.

Jim and Eric were already halfway back to the bikes, talking among themselves, when Sam and Willy started back.

"That was massively uncool," said Willy. "You should try to make it up to him."

Sam just sulked. They caught up to the guys just as Jim started to put his clothes back on. Eric waited silently by his bike.

Willy went up to Eric. "You guys aren't leaving, are you? We all just got here. We're not going to go now, after everything?" Sam just sat down next to his bike and wouldn't even look at them.

"I think it would be best to go," Jim said sullenly. "I think Eric really wants to go." Willy knew that this could be it for the day, for the whole weekend, if they all left mad. He had to try to talk everyone out of this.

CHOICE ⇒

If the guys listen, turn to page 19.

If the guys don't listen, turn to page 114.

OK," said Willy. "I'll ask Jim about Eric."

Sam nodded in agreement. Without a word more, the two headed straight for Jim.

"Jim!" Willy called out. Jim and Eric stopped what they were doing and looked back. "Can I talk to you for a second?"

Sam passed Willy and said, "Hey Eric, let me show you around the factory," and they both disappeared into the building.

Jim looked around uncomfortably. They heard hollow thuds as Eric and Sam rummaged around in the basement. After a moment Jim looked back at Willy. "What's this all about? Why so secretive?"

"It's not for me so much as it is for Sam, but we're kind of curious about Eric." Jim looked down at his feet and kicked at the ground, but he didn't say anything. "All we want to know is a little about the guy, and you seem to be the one who knows him."

"What?"

"Who is he? How do you know him? What's up with what's in his pocket?"

Jim leaned against the building with a pained expression on his face. "I really can't tell you that much about Eric. The school nurse and the principal asked me to be quiet and just show Eric some fun over here in Millersburg."

"At least tell me what he's hiding in his pocket. Is it a weapon, or . . . what?"

Jim looked at his feet for a long time, then said uneasily, "It's a thing about Eric I can't tell you about. I found it out about him in gym class. He's excused from it permanently, so I followed him around to see why. It's a thing I saw, and he found out."

"You're not going to tell me, are you?" Willy asked.

"I wish I could, but I don't think it's right. He'll tell you when he's ready, if you'll just wait." Jim smiled and shook his head. "He's really not a bad guy. You wouldn't believe it, but he's got a killer imagination. He comes up with the coolest scenarios, but only after you get to know him. He's just too embarrassed to ever say anything that anyone can hear."

"He just seems weird to me." Willy looked down and shook his head. "Look, Jim," he said impatiently, grabbing Jim's arm, "we've been friends longer than you've known Eric, and you know you can trust me, so why don't you tell me and I'll keep it a secret."

Jim looked away for a second, then turned back. "Well . . ."

CHOICE ⇒

If Jim tells, turn to page 44.

If Jim doesn't tell, turn to page 14.

"Look," said Willy, "I'm the one who saw the guy, and I'm the one who ran into him. There's no way he'll come after all of us. I say we just go back and see where he is and what he's doing." The others one by one shrugged their shoulders and said, "OK, Willy, you saw the guy."

"OK, this is what we need to do. Hide everything in case we need to make a quick escape and can't grab it on the way out."

The Ringers and Eric ditched the red backpack over by the fence where they came in and leaned their bikes there, ready to take off quickly if they had to.

"I don't know if this sounds like a good idea," Jim cautioned.

"OK then, Jim," Willy said, "you be a lookout. You stay here and whistle if you see anyone."

"OK." Then Jim turned and walked toward the front gate.

"Eric!" barked Willy.

Eric jumped.

"You come with us. We'll need at least three scouts."

The three scouts headed off toward the entrance of the woods. It was only about forty yards from the main gate, an easy distance to run. They crouched by a hill, one of the larger ones that was about six yards tall.

After settling in under a clump of weeds, the three

scouts looked toward the entrance of the woods. Nothing moved. Just inside, they could see a wheel from Willy's bike, its chrome standing out against the dark green weeds.

"Look, Willy, there's your bike." Sam pointed to the wheel. "Or at least part of it. Do you think he left it there as bait?"

"You watch too much TV, " Eric mumbled.

Willy looked from Eric to Sam and back again. "What are you guys talking about? The man is probably gone. I got away, remember? And I saw his box." Willy looked back at the opening and squinted his eyes. "He's probably miles away from here by now."

"Yeah, right," Sam agreed.

"Listen, guys," Eric said, "I have a plan." Willy was surprised that Eric would offer a plan after saying so little all day. "The first thing we have to do is see if the guy is in there. We need to gather as many rocks as we can and throw them in the woods to try to flush him out, or at least make some noise. If we stand in three places: there, and there, and there . . ." He pointed with his right hand, the little fingers wiggled practically under Willy's nose. "After about a hundred rocks, we should be able to tell if the guy's still there."

Sam and Jim sat and thought about the plan for a while.

"It sounds OK," Willy finally said. "You guys go get rocks and get in your places. We'll do it in five minutes."

The boys gathered armloads of rocks and went to their places. Willy raised his arm and waited for the guys to nod their heads. They both did, and he dropped his arm. A

barrage of rocks flew into the woods. None of the guys
made a sound at first, but after a few dozen rocks they
started to scream with excitement. Everywhere the leaves
in the woods danced in a hail of rocks. Eric and Sam just
threw wildly, but Willy knew just where to throw them.
Except for their own screams, they didn't hear a noise from
the woods.

After about five minutes, they ran out of rocks. Willy
waved the other two over, and they crouched behind the
clump.

"I think he must be gone," Eric whispered.

"Let's go up and take a look," Willy said. "Reload." The
guys each picked up a couple more rocks and advanced on
the woods. They looked in carefully, ready to jump and run
at the slightest noise. Willy's bike was at the entrance. The
bike looked fine, except for a few nicks in the paint where
they had hit it with their own rock barrage. "Oh, no," Willy
sighed, then he felt a sigh of resolution in himself. He
continued ahead, but a little more recklessly. As they crept
deeper into the woods they could see the rocks they had
thrown lying about everywhere.

Deep in the woods they found a hump in the leaves.
It looked like a blanket, or a gray jacket that was covered
with leaves. They crept closer and carefully removed the
blanket. It covered the box that Willy had tripped on. To
their complete surprise, it was full of valuable items: tape
players, wallets, jewelry, and even rolls of money.

Without a word, the guys lifted the box and started
to head for the entrance of the woods. They looked
guiltily at each other as they walked. "We aren't going to

steal it; we're just going to look at it," Willy said to make them all feel better. Willy imagined he could hear the white-haired man about to pounce on them, but the woods were silent.

Out by the hill they peered inside the box. It was full of stuff. Willy looked up with surprise to see that Eric had brought out Willy's bike.

They hurried out to the entrance, where they found Jim sitting in the bushes by the fence. As they came up to him, he jumped out and started whispering quickly, "He came out! He came out!"

"What happened?"

"After you left, the man came out. He walked right past me and went up the street. I think he's in that ratty old house," Jim said triumphantly, pointing. "Is that the box?"

"Yeah," said Sam. "But what are we gonna do now?"

"The way I see it," Willy said. He spoke with authority now, since everything was going so well. He and Sam were getting cocky. "The way I see it, we keep the box. Finders keepers."

"But that's not ours!" said Jim. "We can't just take the box like it belongs to us. There's a lot of valuable stuff in there! That would be stealing!"

"But he probably stole it from someone else. I think we should take it and show the police."

"Ah, let's just forget the box," said Sam. "This is stupid. The old man is probably homeless and needs this stuff. Let's leave him alone and motocross."

"Sam's right," said Jim.

"I say we case the house. Let's go up to the factory

and see if he comes back," Eric suggested, trying to win points with Willy.

If they decide to return the box, turn to page 6.

If they decide to case the house, turn to page 65.

A trip to the Pits, the Sinks, or the old run-down factory .... An old man on a motocross course.... A box.... The Vipers! What does it all have in common? And what does it all have to do with the Ringers?

If you haven't already figured it all out, start again and follow the Ringers around from choice to choice. See where else their curiosity leads them ... and *misleads* them!

And don't miss the other Ringer adventures. They've been many places—and in many fixes—with each other, with new friends, with their God. You'll have fun making choices for them ... and seeing where they lead!

142

R. P. Proctor
has a Master's degree in creative writing.

*If you enjoy **Choice Adventures**, you'll
want to read these exciting series from
Tyndale House Publishers!*

McGee and Me!
#1 The Big Lie
#2 A Star in the Breaking
#3 The Not-So-Great Escape
#4 Skate Expectations
#5 Twister & Shout
#6 Back to the Drawing Board
#7 Do the Bright Thing
#8 Take Me Out of the Ball Game
#9 'Twas the Fight before Christmas
#10 In the Nick of Time
#11 The Blunder Years
#12 Beauty in the Least

Anika Scott
#1 The Impossible Lisa Barnes
#2 Tianna the Terrible
#3 Anika's Mountain
#4 Ambush at Amboseli
#5 Sabrina the Schemer

Spindles
#1 The Mystery of the Missing Numbat
#2 The Giant Eagle Rescue

You can find Tyndale books at fine bookstores everywhere.
If you are unable to find these titles at your local bookstore,
you may write for ordering information to:

**Tyndale House Publishers
Tyndale Family Products Dept.
Box 448
Wheaton, IL 60189**